BEAUTY'S WAR

GODS REBORN, BOOK ONE

ANNA EDWARDS
CLAIRE MARTA

Copyright © 2018 by Anna Edwards & Claire Marta

All rights reserved. No part of this publication may be reproduced, distributed or transmitted in any form or by any means, without prior written permission.

www.clairemartawritesbooks.wordpress.com

www.AuthorAnnaEdwards.com

This is a work of fiction. Names, characters, places, and incidents are a product of the author's imagination. Locales and public names are sometimes used for atmospheric purposes. Any resemblance to actual people, living or dead, or to businesses, companies, events, institutions, or locales is completely coincidental.

Warning: This book contains sexually explicit scenes and adult language and may be considered offensive to some readers. This book is for sale to adults only, as defined by the laws of the country in which you made your purchase.

Disclaimer: Please do not try any sexual practice without the guidance of an experienced practitioner. Neither the publisher nor the author will be responsible for any loss, harm, injury, or death resulting from the use of the information contained in this book.

Cover Design by www.CharityHendry.com

Editing by Tracy Roelle

Formatting by Anna Edwards

Proofreading by Sheena Taylor

Beauty's War/ Anna Edwards Claire Marta -- 1st ed.

ISBN-13-978-1718095397

The Gods Reborn series is based on Roman Theology. There are many different stories surrounding what really happened with the God's and especially who is the father of whom. While we've tried to stick to accuracy, it's not always been possible. We hope you keep that in mind when reading.

Anna & Claire.

BLURB

Vicky thought she knew who she was — a young woman from Devon, England with a love of drawing. However, a trip to Rome reveals there are ancient forces at work, which she never knew existed. Beauty in her world is dying. Can a handsome stranger save her from the encroaching darkness and allow her to find her true self before it is too late?

Mars is the God of War and Masculinity. If he wants something, he takes it, that is the force he wields in a world blinded to his existence. The enemy has arrived, and a war is coming. Can he find the control he needs to overcome evil or will his feelings toward a human woman bring him to his knees?

The power of the gods and their eternal battle of good vs. evil is about to be unleashed on an unsuspecting world. Is it possible for Mars to reawaken Venus before the God of the Underworld captures them in his deadly trap?

Beauty's War is a dark modern day, fantasy, paranormal romance based upon Roman mythology.

You shouldn't always believe the history you were taught, because the reality may be something completely unexpected.

"As we wander, grieving, in yet another dark moment, amid our pain we must struggle to remember the redemptive power of love and hope."

Ephraim Mirvis

MARS
Chapter one

"Bloody arrogant assholes. Motherfucking cocksuckers." I barge through the main entry doors of my firm and stomp loudly along the marble foyer muttering to myself the entire time. "Waste of my fucking time, I should take my favorite spear and stick it so far up their asses when they open their mouths you'll be able to see the tip. I'll show them for making me look a fool. They don't call me the God of War for no reason." I'm still bemoaning my fate when I get to the top floor of the building. It houses the directors of the law firm I work for—my father's firm, and he's Jupiter, the King of Gods. I slam into my office and slump down into my comfortable leather chair. A few seconds later, the door opens, and my father stands there. He's dressed, as always, in a superbly tailored pinstripe suit. His salt and pepper hair is immaculately styled. He shows no sign of the stress I do. I bet if I looked in the mirror my tie would be wonky, and my chestnut brown hair all over the place as though I'd been caught in a blizzard.

"Didn't go well, then?" He smirks at me. I resist the urge to slam my fist into his face. It doesn't seem to go down well with my father when I feel the need to flex my muscles in this way. Especially if it involves his face. Last time I did it, he banished me to Tartarus for a month to think about my misdemeanor. It really wasn't as much fun as it sounds like it should be.

"Pluto had his sniveling little underling, Orcus, there. The conniving little runt got the bastard, Marco, off. All charges were dropped. And to add insult to injury, the judge called me forward and said if I couldn't set out a better case in the future, then I should reconsider my profession." I put my head in my hands and groan. I can still see the smug smile on the defendant's face when the judge brought her hammer down and told him he was free to go. The man was a killer, a cold-blooded murderer, who prayed on young women. He would take them back to his lair, strip them, and bind them with chains. He'd starve them for days until they were crazy with hunger, and then he'd rape them repeatedly before peeling the skin from their bodies while they died in agony. I had to look through thousands of pictures he took. How the judge found him innocent is beyond me. The guy had sold his soul to Pluto and his team. I hope he'll enjoy the rest of eternity in the underworld with them. I just hope the poor hopeless souls he murdered have found some peace up in the clouds of heaven.

My father comes closer to my desk. I hear his heavy footsteps on the tiled floor. He places his hand on my back.

"You did everything you could for those girls. We can't fight the darker side of our profession, not until we are stronger. Pluto has the power now."

I sit upright in my chair and rub my temples.

"We have to stop him. I hear it every day. The cries of war. It's agonizing. I'm in so much pain all the time."

My father perches on the desk.

"I hear it as well. You have to switch it off; it's the only way to function."

"I can't. I'm the God of War, Father. It calls to me."

"Don't let it."

My struggle is daily and all too real. The Roman gods have been around since the inception of the Earth. We used to rule in the heavens, worshipped by the people, but over time, it changed, and we were forced into hiding. My father started up the law firm we work in, trying to help humanity. Unfortunately, Pluto, the God of the Underworld, set up a rival firm and uses his position to further his desire to turn the inhabitants of the world against each other. Many of the gods have forgotten who they are and have, for all intents and purposes, become humans. Their powers suppressed by a world full of darkness, hatred, violence, and suffering. They age, die, and are reborn, walking this Earth for eternity without the knowledge of who they are. As well as trying to prevent savages, like this rapist and murderer, get away with crimes, the firm is also a front for trying to find these human gods before Pluto does. My father and brother, Hercules, head up that division of our firm while my Aunt Juno and I run the front of a solicitor's firm. We're finding too often, though, the sides are clashing. One of the women killed was later discovered to be a goddess. We lost her; she's reborn again somewhere on this planet, and we have no hope of finding her or knowing what damage a brutal murder has done to her sub-consciousness.

"Maybe I should go back up to the heavens for a while. It could be my presence on this planet is creating so much evil.

Everyone senses the thirst for blood that comes from war and looks at how they can use it to create chaos."

"No." My father's voice booms. "You're integral here, Mars. I'll not see you hide away with your tail between your legs. You're an exceptional lawyer. The judge was probably on Pluto's payroll. She treated you the way she did to make you look bad. Persephone will return to the underworld soon for her six months down there. Pluto will spend as little time on the surface as he can, then. He'll be too interested in torturing his concubine. That'll be our time to strike. Orcus hangs off every word of Pluto's. He won't be able to control the firm without his mentor there. We just have to bide our time."

My father looks over the pile of folders on my desk. They're cases I have coming up. They should all be easy wins as the defendants are monsters, but after today, I'm not holding out much hope for a victory in any of them.

"Why don't we swap you and Hercules around for a bit. He's growing weary of searching daily for human gods and wants to spend a little more time with his wife. You've been tied to this office twenty-four seven, recently. I'm sure you have physical needs clouding your judgment as well."

I roll my eyes.

"If you're asking about Bellona, then no, I've not seen her in a few weeks." Bellona is my adopted sister and Goddess of War. I know my father would love nothing more than for us to join together and create a formidable force, but it's not like that between us. She's not the person who captures my heart. We're friends with benefits as the humans like to say. Mind you, as Roman gods, we're a highly sexual bunch, and many of us have associates we often end up balls deep in: male or female no discrimination.

"Then go see her? Have a think on what I've said about swapping with Hercules for a while. A fresh pair of eyes in each department makes sense. It could give us the advantage we need to beat Pluto."

"No, I think the word you're looking for there is called a miracle."

"We're gods; we can create them."

I snort a sound of defeat.

"I think we've all forgotten how to produce them it's been so long."

Jupiter slides from my desk and picks up the pile of legal documents.

"Father?" I wearily question.

"No arguments. Go. Take the rest of the day off. I'll deal with these for now until you've had a rest."

"Thank you, "I offer with loving affection to my father. We may have had our fights over the years, and our disagreements have threatened to change the course of history, but I know he wants what's best for both the world and his children, no matter who the mother is. He leaves, and I sit back in my chair and shut my eyes. When I open them, I'm outside Bellona's Tuscan villa on the outskirts of Florence. One of the perks of being a god is that we can just shut our eyes and think of a location and the magic that surrounds us will take us there. I knock, and she answers almost immediately. She's wearing a long floaty white dress. It looks almost like one of the togas we're famed for wearing but more modern.

"Mars." She presses a kiss to my lips, and I respond with warmth. "It's been far too long."

"I'm sorry, Bel, I've been busy. A pretty nasty case."

"You win?" she asks with enthusiasm and leads me into a living room overlooking the vineyard hills of the region.

When I look sheepishly at the floor and don't answer, she instantly changes the subject.

"I'll get you some wine and olives. I've just picked the last of the harvest, and the wine's local."

"I'm not hungry or thirsty, thank you." The look crossing her face tells me she knows exactly why I'm here. I'm not just the God of War, I'm also the God of Masculinity. It's left me highly sexually charged. I need to get my dick wet often. It helps me function. When I find release, my endorphins are spread throughout the world. I literally invite people to make love, not war. My current mood is probably causing the upsurge of violence in the world, so I need to put a stop to it.

"What do you want me to do?" Bellona licks her lips and comes to stand directly in front of me. She places a hand on my broad chest. I'm still dressed in my formal suit from the court.

"Let's start with you sucking me off to spread a bit of peace in the world, if even for only a few moments, and then we'll see where the evening takes us." I raise an eyebrow cockily at her. She knows full well I can go all night and not need a rest in between. You'll never hear her complaining, though. She likes sex just as much as I do. Must be the juxtaposition of love and hate—make love not war, and all that crap humans spout just before they go and bomb or shoot someone.

Bellona moves from where she is standing in front of me to a sofa and collects a silk cushion from it. She returns to me and places it down on the marbled floor and kneels.

"I won't be gentle," I warn her. "I want you to take all of me. You don't swallow until I say."

"Our relationship has never been about tender lovemaking, Mars. It doesn't suit either of us," she replies while undoing my belt, pulling the zipper of my dress pants down, and freeing my already hard cock. She strokes her hand up and down the length a few times before guiding it into her mouth. I feel my body instantly relax after the stresses of the day. The urge to maim, destroy, and kill leaving me just because I've sunk my dick into a warm and welcoming vessel. She runs her tongue over my tip, and I hiss. Damn, she gives good head, but tonight, she's not quick enough. I need more; I need to take pleasure for myself, so I twist my hand around the long braid she's tied her blond hair in. I pull it back hard, and my dick pops from her mouth. She whimpers in a little discomfort, but her eyes sparkle with her own arousal.

"Don't forget, I'm in charge here, cara mia. I'm going to use that pretty little mouth of yours to rid myself of the voices in my head." Her response has my dick jumping from joy because she submits to me entirely and opens her mouth wider. It's the go-ahead I need to fuck her face and get myself off. I use the hair twisted around my hand to pull her backward and forward over my length. Contrary to popular belief, and all the statues in the famous museums, gods are very well endowed, and every time I bring her lips to my hilt, she beautifully gags. The sound turns me on even more, and before long, my balls are tightening, and the hot stream of my release is rushing down my length and into her mouth. She's choking on me but not swallowing. Bellona obeys my rules always, for she knows I'm superior to her. Arrogant I know, but I'm a god, what do you expect!

I still, the tip of my cock resting on her lips. My cum spills out of her mouth and down her chin. I'm breathing heavily. My release was ferocious and much needed. I listen for the voices in my head, and I can see by the way her eyes go black Bellona is doing the same. Battle cries are silenced, no war, just the erotic call of thousands finding release from pent up stresses and frustrations. I savor the beautiful melody; it's a symphony to the world and should be the only tune that's ever played. It doesn't last, though, for in the background, the cries of pain and suffering resurface like the horses pounding through Funeralia in Liszt's famous piece of music, Armonie Poetiche e Religiose.

I cry out in sympathy for the suffering in the world. Bellona wails. Tears tumble down her cheeks as the voices return to her head.

"Swallow," I command. She does so. I'll use her to take the torment of my emotions, entwined so intimately with my sexuality, and bury them deep inside her. We'll beat Pluto and his men. We'll save the human gods and make all right in the world again. If only it were that simple.

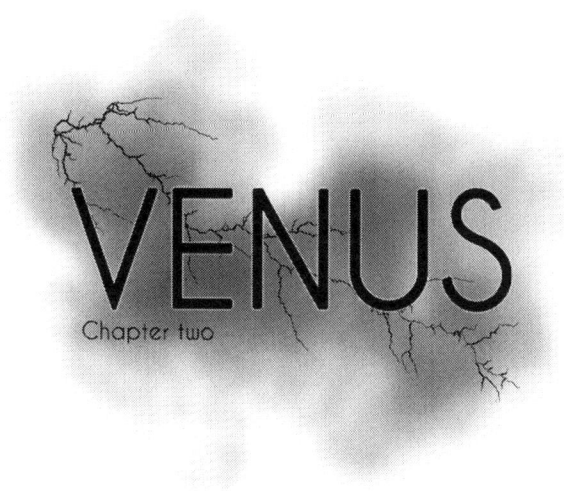

VENUS
Chapter two

Groaning softly, I stretch, trying to relieve the crick in my neck. The heat of the afternoon Rome sun adds to the discomfort, leaving a fine sheen of sweat over my body.

I know I should move. I've been in the same position for hours, but I don't want to lose the moment. Staring down at the sketch I know it's worth it. The Coliseum, in all its ancient glory before me, is mirrored in every stroke of my pencil. Beautiful, a monument to a time long past dead. With an absent brush of my hand, I pull back the loose tendrils of platinum blonde locks, which have escaped my messy ponytail at the nape of my neck and loop them behind my ear.

My gaze follows the lines, and dipping, I add a little more shading, letting my pencil drift across the paper, bringing it more to life. It's a piece of work I know I'm going to keep. Anything else I produce here, I'll happily sell in my art studio back in Devon. My normal seascapes and rustic paintings do well, but with something as exotic as the scenes here, I know they'll do even better.

"Vicky, are you done yet?" Susan's voice is laced with irritation. My best friend loves my work but has no patience waiting for me to finish. Not that I can blame her. Twenty-four hours into our first day on holiday and I haven't been able to resist getting my sketchbook out.

"I'm done," I tell her, flipping the book closed.

Looking up, I find her rounded cheeks flushed from the heat. Her normally curly auburn hair is frizzy from the change in climate, framing her pretty freckled face. Decked out in cream shorts and a yellow t-shirt, her sandals give the finishing touch to her holiday look.

"Good! You've been hunched over that forever and missing all the surrounding things."

The murmurs of the crowd filter back into my awareness. Bright colors of people wandering along enjoying the scenery and the summer afternoon. Lost, as I was drawing, I haven't been aware of how busy the place has gotten. It's always the way when I'm being creative. Since stepping off the plane, a sense of peace has enveloped me. I've never been somewhere that feels so familiar. An echo in my soul as if I've been here before. It's a weird experience to feel at home among strangers in a foreign land.

Stuffing my book and pencils back in my backpack, I gingerly rise to my feet. A cramp makes me moan as it knifes up my legs, the long white cotton skirt I'm wearing swirling to my ankles. As fit as I am it never helps.

Susan chuckles, amused at my pain. "Let's find a pizzeria. I'm starving, and the pizza here's amazing."

She's done nothing but eat since we got here. Not that I'm complaining, the food is fantastic and far better than anything Italian we have back home. We'll both be on a diet when the holiday is finished.

Bag resting on my shoulder, I tuck my other arm through hers. "Did I ever tell you that you're bossy?"

"All the time, but you love me for it."

My grin matches hers. "Who would have thought we'd ever be rambling around Rome on a girl's holiday?"

With a tug, she gets us walking in the direction of some restaurants nestled at the end of a street in the distance. "It was about bloody time. We both needed a break from Devon. Don't get me wrong, I love our village, but nothing ever happens there." We're both used to a quiet life. This is more excitement than we've had in years. It's fun. An adventure we won't forget in a hurry. "And so far, I'm enjoying everything about Italy." She continues, returning a flirty smile to a couple of tanned, good looking males as they pass us by.

Swatting her hand, I grab her attention. "Hey, no guys, remember, that was the deal."

I can already feel the beads of sweat crawling down beneath the loose blue cotton t-shirt I'm wearing. The only escapes are the air-conditioned shops or our hotel room.

"Yes, I know," Susan grumbles with a regretful sigh. "It doesn't mean I can't admire them, though."

A ten-minute walk and we're at a busy touristy place. Rome is full of them. All catering for people on the go as they sightsee and relax. There's an old-world charm about the place. Crowded tables, with checkered red and white table cloths, bustling with hungry patrons. Waiters, sweeping past, juggle plates with a long-practiced ease only earned over time. Catching the eye of one, we're directed toward a table in a corner. It's out of the way. Intimate. A place we can people watch without being noticed. Something I've always loved to do.

Dropping my bag by my feet, I rest my chin on the heel of

my hand, elbow on the table. Slowly, I examine the crowd. So many faces. All different ages and to my artist's eye, I see so many possibilities. Each one has a story to tell. Fingers itching to draw, I resisted the urge. Not everyone likes to be immortalized on paper. It's something I've learned from experience. Susan would also kill me.

"Margarita?" she suggests as she leafs through the menu. "I just adore how the cheese is melted, and those fresh tomatoes are to die for, and we'll get some local wine."

"Sounds good," I agree absently, my attention sweeping back to her only to be hooked on something on a table further down.

Dark, handsome, the man's features are more breathtaking than I've ever seen before. He's more beautiful than any painting or sculpture. There's a strength to him that's more than skin deep. A power that radiates from within. Strong square jaw, cleanly shaved, his looks put every other male in the place to shame. Lips firm and kissable, he bears the Mediterranean allure. A sexy sensuality in every line of his muscled frame beneath his expensive business suit. Déjà vu hits me hard. He's so familiar, but I know he has a face I would never forget. There's no way we've met before. If we had, I know he would have been unforgettable. Boisterously loud, his laughter when he throws back his head and chuckles sends a primitive need right down to my feminine core. I find myself transfixed. Mesmerized with an ache just to reach out and touch him. Watching the muscles work in his throat as he takes a drink, a shaky breath escapes me.

"Vicky are you ok? Your cheeks are really flushed." Susan's voice barely registers. "I think you got a little too much sun."

Unable to reply, I just keep staring. Why can't I stop? It's like my eyes have a mind of their own. My body heats up, and I know it has nothing to do with the summer weather. How can one guy send my libido spinning? Squirming in place, I press my thighs together to alleviate the hunger that's pulsing in my pussy.

"Earth to Vicky." A hand wiggling in my face snaps me from my daze. Susan frowns at me, her large brown eyes troubled. "Are you ok?"

Looking down, I realize our pizzas and drinks have arrived. "Yes, sorry, I got a bit distracted." With a more than an obvious glance over her shoulder, my friend scopes out the source of my drooling.

"Holy shit, that guy's hot," she mutters. "No wonder you spaced out. Maybe he's a model or something. He sure has the looks."

Scooping up a slice from my plate, I keep my gaze down. There's no way I want to get sucked in to whatever just happened before. Thank god, he never caught me staring. Warmth blooms in my cheeks just at the thought. He's probably here with his wife or girlfriend. Not that I noticed anyone else at his table. No, I'm just sat here gawking like a freaking idiot.

Munching on the end of my pizza, I can't stop the small moan of delight. I'll definitely miss this, along with all the sights when we fly home in six days' time.

"He's looking over," Susan suddenly hisses as she twists back round to face me, her excitement clear.

My eyes flick up. I can't help it. Breath stuttering in my lungs, I find my gaze locked with a pair of deep pools of chocolate brown. They're so deep, so intense, I find myself trapped. Hunger flashes across his face and just as suddenly vanishes beneath an icy look of reserve.

One second I'm a prisoner, the next I'm free of his stare. It's only then I realize I'm still holding a slice of half eaten pizza against my lips. My other hand has a death grip on the edge of the table so tight my knuckles are white. Loosening my grasp, I let go of the surface.

"What the fuck just happened?" Susan whispers between bites of her food. "That was like...I don't know what, but the whole atmosphere in the place changed. It was kind of hot and weird all at the same time."

Discarding the slice, I curl my fingers around my glass. After that, I need a drink or two.

"I don't know," I managed to croak before lifting my drink and taking a long gulp. The fruity flavored wine is welcome. Something to settle my nerves. What appetite I had has deserted me. Everything inside me is a jumble. I don't know why. How can one look affect me so much? Who is he? Some business man in for an early lunch? Passing through Rome, maybe on pleasure. Chancing a peek, I see his back is to me. His shoulders are so broad, giving a woman something to cling to when her legs are wrapped around his lean, perfect hips.

An image of tanned, muscular limbs entwined with my paler ones' flashes through my head. His body covering mine as he takes me over and over. I almost groan, hearing his imaginary masculine moans of satisfaction while his cock slides into me. Sipping more wine, I'm on the verge of having an orgasm at the table as the erotic fantasy continues to reel through my head. What the hell is wrong with me?

"Oh my god, what if he comes over?" Susan whispers.

Just the thought has my breathing turn shallower. Observing him at a distance is one thing, but I'm not sure my body would cope with seeing him up close. Movement catches my eye. For a second, I hold my breath expectantly. However, tall, confident, and without even a backward glance, the stranger stalks toward the door and out onto the street. Relief floods me, but the disappointment is sharp, and I'm not sure why. For a second, he pauses. He doesn't turn just stops, and then in a heartbeat, he vanishes into the passing traffic.

Tension oozes from my shoulders. I feel drained, yet still oddly restless and uneasy. Whoever he is, he invokes lust and fear in equal measure. He may be gone, but I know his features are something that strangely are going to haunt me.

MARS
Chapter three

I materialize back in my office and lean against the knotted oak desk before inhaling sharply. There was no doubt the woman I've just been watching is a goddess. The power surrounding her was overwhelming. When she looked directly at me, I felt none of the war I usually have waging in my head, only peace and love. It had taken my breath away, and I had to leave before I went over to her, bent her over the table and sunk my cock deep within her.

My father had given the names of three people that I needed to investigate as potential human gods. The first two men showed no signs, if they had any powers it was so far hidden in their psyche that it was lost forever. The final girl, however, she was an entirely different story.

"Any luck?" My father walks into my office unannounced. He has a habit of doing that.

"I can remove two men from the list, but I think the girl's a definite possibility."

My father cocks his head to the side as he regards me.

"What's wrong?"

"Nothing." I shake my head.

"Mars?" It's the authoritative tone of my childhood. The one that had me freeze when I was caught stealing the last cookie from the tin. My now strong form doesn't reflect the number of times I was caught doing it.

"She's powerful. I only just made it away without causing a scene?" I reluctantly answer.

"Scene?"

"Fuck her in the middle of a packed restaurant."

He nods. "Yes, that would have caused quite the commotion, which we don't need." My father takes a seat. "Does she have any idea of what she is?"

I shake my head.

"Pluto?"

"I didn't see him or any of his cronies. Doesn't mean that they aren't on to her, though. She exudes power. It wouldn't surprise me if there were a bright neon beacon above her, flashing that she was a goddess. That was the power passed between us when she looked into my eyes. Pluto or Orcus will feel her and find her soon."

"You need to go back and protect her. It's too soon to tell her what she is. We have to take it slowly. The women are always the emotional ones."–he rolls his eyes– "Befriend her."

"Lie to her you mean." I snort with derision.

"You tell her outright what she is, and she'll run and alert herself to Pluto. She'll think you're insane."

"Even if I show her what I can do?" I hold my arm out, and in a puff of smoke, a sharp metal spear appears within my hand.

My father chuckles.

"Your brother tried that once; it didn't go down well."–He winces– "Nasty incident, spears really aren't meant to go where the sun doesn't shine."

I force my spear to vanish into mid-air and shudder. "He never told me that." I chuckle.

"You would've teased him."

"Hell, yes I would have."

"That's exactly why you weren't told." My father looks up at me with frustration. "Befriending her is the only way. She has to trust you before you can tell her what she is."

"Fine," I agree. I don't particularly like lying. It goes against my whole nature as a lawyer. Well, actually that isn't true. As a solicitor, I lie most days to get people acquitted of crimes they've so obviously committed and have no remorse for, but that's why I'm one of the best.

"I'll put the standard observation on her, but the rest is up to you. If she's as powerful as you say, then we can't afford to lose her. We lost Minerva to Pluto, recently. I've no idea what she's suffering at his hands, but I won't rest until I find her. This woman could be one of the powerful goddesses we're still missing. She could help us bring peace and more stability to Rome. You've said yourself that the gods we've found, thus far, are the ones of chaos. War rages inside your head. It has no balance in this world, yet. There's no sense of wisdom and love to counteract the hatred."

"Venus?" I interrupt.

"You sensed a great power. If she's your equal in this fight, then it will affect you."

"I'll do all I can to protect her." I stand up taller and place my hand on my heart. It's a vow between us both: unspoken truths in the vehemence of the declaration.

My father waves his hand to dismiss me, and I dissipate

only to reform where I feel the girl strongest. She invades my every pore when I reappear into the warm evening air of Rome. The city is still bustling with people, heading to dinner or back home after sampling the delights of pizza and pasta. The variety of languages I can hear are as big a cacophony as the ones that flood my head from around the world when I choose to let the cries in. American's, with a rich twang, call out about the beauty of the city, the British bemoan the fact that the weather isn't this warm back home, and Japanese tourists talk loudly into live videos about what they're seeing. The odd Italian dialect captures my ear with discussions about what delightful food they'll sample tonight. I chuckle as a French couple walk past, and he declares his undying love for his partner only for her to blush and tell him to save it for the bedroom. As much as I like listening to the characters of the city, I have a job to do. Looking around, I spot the woman from earlier with her friend. They're by the Spanish Steps, and she's hunched over a pad of paper, feverishly sketching. Her friend is chatting animatedly to two gentlemen. I don't need to be a god to understand what they're thinking while talking to the girl. It's evident from the bulge in both their jeans.

Befriend her, my father said. I can do that. It's not like I'm the God of War or anything, and people cower in fear at my presence. Have I mentioned lately that I can be an arrogant and demanding sod at times? It's in my nature, can't help it, and won't ever change.

Talk to her. Say hi. That's how people start up conversations, isn't it? Right. Fuck! I'm no good at this. Which is why my father typically sends Hercules to do this sort of thing. He's all long, beautiful flowing hair and stunning looks. Plus, he can bench press half of the people sitting on these steps with one finger. I can probably do that, but I'd start a fight by even trying. A woman pushes a man and tells him to, 'get lost'. He accuses her of cheating on him, and she responds by saying that if he can't trust her, then their relationship is over. I groan loudly, forgetting I'm pretty much standing directly behind the woman from earlier. She looks up at the commotion and then around to me. Her eyes widen like a rabbit in headlights.

"Hi." She squeaks and quickly looks around for her friend who's taken a seat with the two men chatting her up.

"Ciao," I respond trying to play it cool, but the second she'd looked at me, I could feel her power again. It captures me in a cocoon, making me want to act like a rambling idiot and fall at her feet in worship. I swallow deeply. "Nice picture." I nod my head toward the drawing she has open in her sketchbook.

"It's the steps," she replies, and her cheeks blush bright red. I hear her mutter under her breath about the 'stating the obvious' reply. "Way to play it cool, Vicky. Just look like a right idiot in front of the hot man."

"They're good. I like the fact that you don't have a lot of details on the people, just the movement of them coming and going." Her picture's actually pretty good. It looks like the crowd is in motion.

"Thank you." She blushes again.

"You were in the restaurant earlier." I try to be to the point, now, hoping it'll put her at ease.

"I was. Great food, my first proper Italian pizza."

"I'm glad you like it. That restaurant is one of my favorites."

"Really?"–She looks me up and down– "You don't look

much like a pizza and pasta man." "Damn it," she hisses under her breath. "Stop being such a dork."

"I get a lot of exercise."

She opens and closes her mouth like a fish, and I can see she isn't sure how to respond to my comment. It was actually meant perfectly innocently, but given her mind is apparently in the gutter when she looks at me, its sexual connotations haven't gone unnoticed.

We go silent. I look over at her friend. The two men she's with are starting to get a bit handsy with her. She's trying to get up and away from them.

"What's your friend's name?" I ask. The artist who I now know to be Vicky, thanks to her mumbling, turns her head toward her friend.

"Susan," she replies with worry in her voice.

"Susan, bambina," I shout and wink at her. The other woman looks up at the sound of her name, the two guys follow her gaze. "Sorry I'm late, you coming or not? I'm ready for that threesome you and blondie here promised me."

Everyone sitting nearby stops their conversations and looks at us. The two guys pale when I puff myself up to full stature. I'm twice the size of both of them put together. God's have great genes.

"Handsome," Susan calls back. "I thought you'd left us." In two seconds, she's up and away from the other two men. She's breathless and frightened. I can feel it coming from every pore. As she gets closer, she places her arm through mine. Vicky has quickly packed up her art equipment and slung her bag over her shoulders. She too tucks her arm into mine.

"You're just rescuing my friend, right?" she asks as we

turn away from the Spanish Steps and slip down through the street of Via dei Condotti. "You aren't taking us for a real threesome."

Susan chuckles and squeezes my arm. "I don't know, a threesome with him seems better than with those two perverts. Do you know what they said to me?"

"Keep walking." I groan inwardly. The heat coming from where Vicky has her skin against mine is burning. We finally reach the other end of the street and safety. I pull away from both of the women and rub my scalded arm. "You should be careful who you talk you. I'm afraid there are people around who like to pray on the tourists even in public places." I frown at the auburn-haired girl.

"Sorry," she says while twirling a strand of hair around her finger. I look down at my watch. It's only ten pm, but something tells me that these two will be safer back in their hotel.

"Are you staying far from here?"

"We're having a threesome?" Susan squeals in delight.

"No, we're not." Vicky quickly jumps into the conversation, breaking her silence since we left the steps. "Mr. er, what's your name?"

"Mars." I offer.

"Mr. Mars."

"Just Mars," I cut in.

"Mars was just helping out. Thank you." Vicky looks up at me with her big blue eyes. I'm drawn into them, again. I feel as though I'm floating. Fuck, I hope I'm not since I'm one of the few gods who can fly, and my father told me to make friends with the girl, not freak her out. I look down at my feet, breaking our connection to ensure they're firmly planted on the ground. They are. Phew!

"Thank you, Mars," Susan singsongs to match her friend's gratitude.

"I think it's probably time for you two to return to your hotel for the night. I'll walk you."

"Come in for a nightcap?" Susan offers with a lick of her lips. Vicky jabs her in the rips.

"Hey, just letting him know that if you're going to be a prude, I'm not. He's cute."

"I'll walk you back to your hotel, and then I'll go home," I reply sternly.

"Spoilsport," Susan moans and starts to walk off.

"I'm sorry about her," Vicky apologizes.

"It's not a problem. She seems a handful but harmless."

"She really is. My best friend, and I've known her for what seems like forever."

"It's good to have someone like that." I have friends, actually no, I have consorts who I go to when I need my cocksucked. I've never honestly had that person who wants me for me and not for what I can give them or what services they can provide me.

We fall into step behind Susan. Out of the corner of my eye, I can see Vicky looking up at me. The connection between us is strong, and I can sense that she feels it too. I've never felt such power coming from a goddess before. My father suspects she could be Venus and looking down at her beauty and gracefulness as we walk, I'm starting to believe him. For I know, at this moment, war is very far from my thoughts.

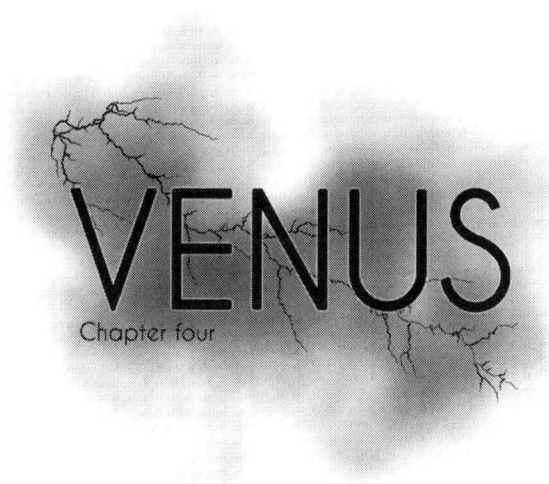

VENUS
Chapter four

My skin prickles at Mars' closeness. With every fiber of my being, I'm aware of every inch of him as he moves beside me. The needy ache is back between my legs. It intensifies with his proximity.

Everything in his appearance screams refined, confident, male.

I still don't know how he found us. In a city as big as Rome, was it really a coincidence we've bumped into him again. Fate?

Susan grins when she catches my gaze. She's enjoying his attention, that's for sure, much more than those creeps she'd run into. I've told her to be careful. Not everyone is as friendly as she thinks they are.

Seeing Mr. tall, dark, and handsome, again, has turned my brain to mush. Tongue darting out to wet my dry lips, I try to think of something to say. Nothing comes to mind. Some hot Italian guy has turned me into a moron. I still can't believe he told everyone we're having a threesome.

Heat scalds my cheeks at the thought. I've never done something like that in my life.

"It was lucky you found us," I babble.

"Yes, it was very fortunate."

I'm barely aware of the odd tourist and Italian passing us by on their way back home. All my focus is on the man at my side. He can't be single. No way in Hell a woman wouldn't have snapped him up already. Then again, maybe he's gay.

Wrinkling my nose, I dump that thought. No. The way he keeps watching me, he's definitely not into guys.

"Well, this is us," Susan announces.

Blinking out of my lusty daze, I realize we're already outside our cheap hotel. I don't remember walking that fast. Not cool. Crap, now I've missed my chance to say something clever or witty.

"You shouldn't wander around so late," Mars advises, holding open the door and ushering us in.

Standing in the shabby foyer, the clerk at the desk eyes our little party.

"You sure you don't want to come up?" Susan persists, running her fingers up to the bulge of his muscular bicep.

Mars looks my way.

His eyes. God, his eyes are hungry again. Just a spark of heat that draws a tiny moan from my throat.

"No," he declines politely. "But tomorrow, I could show you some sights you haven't seen yet, if you'd like. How long are you here for?"

It takes me a second to realize I heard right.

"You want to show us around?" I repeat dumbly.

Mars' expression becomes amused. "With a local, it's the best way to see everything. I can take you places not everyone knows. Let you see the real Rome."

"We'd love to." Susan jumps in before I can speak. "Wouldn't we, Vicky? We're here for the rest of the week."

I nod dumbly. My mind's in the gutter, again, imagining all the things I bet he could show me, which involves getting naked and sweaty. Giving myself a mental slap, I try to stop thinking with my vagina.

"Are you a tour guide? We can pay you for your time," I tell him, common sense finally kicking in.

"No. I'm a lawyer. I have a few days off work, and it'd be more than an honor to show two beautiful women some of my city."

Susan fans herself with her hand, behind him. With a silent look, she indicates I better not fuck this up.

"Why would you do that?" The words are out before I can think.

Mars' eyes light with mischief. "Because I'd like us to be...friends."

Why do I feel like he wants more than that?

"That's very generous of you, but we'll only agree if we can buy you lunch in payment."

There's no way I'll let him do this for free. It's not right.

A charming sexy smile, which almost makes my panties combust, plays across Mars' mouth. "I have a feeling you won't agree until I accept your terms."

Finding the strap of my bag hanging from my shoulder, I curl my fingers around the leather cord. "It doesn't seem right if we don't give you something in return."

"We can always have that threesome," Susan pipes up.

I can't help but roll my eyes. That woman has sex on the brain, right now, and I guess she's not the only one.

"Food," I insist. "You show us around, and we'll feed you."

Cocking his head, Mars surveys my stubborn expression. "You have a deal, Vicky."

I like the way he says my name. How it falls from his lips as if he's savoring it.

"Ok, good. We could meet at around ten tomorrow morning?"

"I'll be here."

Taking my free hand, he raises it to his lips. The brush of his mouth over my knuckles sends my pulse rate rocketing. He lingers for a second as if enjoying the touch of my skin.

Susan looks a little put out when he doesn't take hers but salutes her with a tilt of his head instead.

"Buona Notte, ladies."

As we walk the short distance to the lift, I can feel his eyes on us.

"He's so fucking hot," Susan whispers as we wait for the metal doors to open. "You should've told him to come up."

I don't respond.

He's still watching. I don't need to turn to know he's still there.

As the lift doors whoosh open, I step inside.

Brown eyes hold mine when I turn to face the opening. Mars hasn't moved a muscle from where he left us. He's serious about seeing us safely back, or maybe, he thinks we'll ignore him and go out again.

Only the doors clicking shut breaks the connection.

He's so fucking intense. I've never met a man like him. Someone who commands my whole attention. It's frightening, yet I can't help feeling energized around him.

Releasing a breath, I hadn't realized I was holding, I lean back against the wall. "We aren't inviting him up. We've only just met him."

Susan pouts. "But I want him."

"You've wanted a piece of every male you've seen since we got here," I scold lightly. "We aren't bringing a complete stranger into our room."

"You can't deny you're attracted to him too."

Scrubbing my free hand over my face, I let out a tired sigh. "Yes, he's attractive. Yes, I fancy him, but that doesn't mean I'm just going to jump into bed with him."

I hope I sound convincing. Since we saw him earlier, I have a dozen loose sketches of his features in my notebook pages. He's fast becoming my obsession.

The lift opens, and we both trot out.

"Well, at least we'll get to know him better," Susan points out as she fishes the key to our room from her pocket. "That's a bonus."

Inwardly, I groan.

She's not going to let this go. One way or another, she'll have him upstairs with us. If that happens, will I be able to resist? This is turning out to be a holiday, I have a feeling, we won't forget.

Inside the room, I dump my bag on my single bed.

The place is clean and affordable. It's not the Ritz, but a good place to sleep and change while we explore.

"You can use the bathroom, first." I tell her as I curl up on the mattress. Not waiting for her to reply, I tug my book and pencils from my backpack.

Flipping the pages open, I don't stop until I find the one I desire.

Mars.

Strong, powerful, I've captured his striking profile perfectly. I want something more solid. Not just a hurried drawing, but something I can take my time over. A portrait of the man who has unwittingly become my secret muse.

I'm only half aware of the sound of the shower running muffled behind the closed bathroom door.

Snatching up a pencil, I lose myself in my art. I bring more depth to his features, playing with light and dark. It makes me wish I'd brought my paints. Back home in my studio, I know I'll have more time to bring it to life. A portrait to keep.

It's not like the memory of him will fade. His appearance, voice, and smile have seared themselves like a brand.

"Are you going to get that?"

Susan's voice drags me from my concentration. "Huh?" It's only then, the sound of knocking registers.

Large, fluffy towel wrapped firmly round her body, she hurries to the door.

Hushed voices follow.

I can hear the excitement in her tone. Has Mars returned?

Nervousness clenches my stomach. Oh my god.

Jumping quickly to my feet, I take a few steps toward her only to stop as she turns.

"Vicky, look what's arrived!" Her squeal of happiness is mirrored in the way she bounces toward me.

Behind her, a man wheels in a cart. On top is a bucket, a bottle of champagne nestled in ice. Next to it are two long flute glasses.

"There must be some kind of mistake." I tell the waiter. "We didn't order this."

"With the compliments of the Manager." His smile makes me skin crawl as his beady eyes flick over me.

"Ooh, that's so nice." Grabbing her purse, Susan tugs out a Euro note and pushes it into the guy's hand. "Thank you."

He accepts the tip with a nod, leaving us without a backward glance.

Unease snakes through me. I'm not sure why. The waiter leaves me feeling unsettled.

"Champagne!" Susan wastes no time popping the cork with a giggle.

"Susan, I'm not sure about this," I tell her as she fills the glasses with the golden liquid. "Why would they even send us this up?"

"Maybe, Mars arranged it as a surprise, or they do it for all their guests." She slips one of the drinks into my hand. "Let's just enjoy it."

I stare dubiously down at the alcohol. Would Mars really treat us like this? We've only just met the guy.

"Please," she pleads, eyes imploring. "Can we just have this moment? I know you're going to say drinking it all is going to give us the mother of all hangovers, but a couple of glasses won't hurt."

She's right. I'm being ridiculous. We're here to have fun, and I shouldn't be so uptight. God knows we both need to let our hair down. A week goes fast, and we'll soon be home again with only photos, souvenirs, and memories.

"Alright."

Susan grins. "Cheers."

Clinking our glasses together, we both take a long sip.

It's delicious and decadent. The bubbles tickle my nose as it slides down my throat.

"You should show Mars that sketch,"–Susan tells me as she tops off our drinks– "He'll love it."

Glancing down at the open page still lying on my bed, I shake my head. "No way. He'll think I'm a stalker."

Just the thought of showing him sends heat through my body. Tipping up the glass, I down the contents in one go.

"Vicky, you need to learn to relax. He's into you."

"No, he's just being nice."

Susan snorts in disbelief before finishing off her champagne.

Discarding my own back on the cart, I return to my notebook and pencils. Would he really like it?

Biting my lip, I stare at it with critical eyes. It's not my best work, but it's good. I'm no Michelangelo, but people have always loved what I create. Some clients have told me they find a sense of peace in my paintings, a connection with something calming.

Dizziness hits me so hard I sway.

A thump registers.

I see Susan on the floor. Hair tumbling around her face on the carpet, eyes closed.

"S... Susan?" Her name stutters through my numbing lips.

Pushing up, my legs give out the strength draining out of them as they fold beneath me. Pain jars up my side as I'm greeted by the floor. Everything starts to spin.

What's happening? I don't understand.

As darkness looms a shadow falls over me. The last thing I see before blackness claims me is an unpleasant smile.

MARS
Chapter five

The hairs on the back of my neck stand up, and I know in that instant that something isn't right. Looking around, I sense the evil when I can't even see it amongst the crowd of people returning home after their evening out. Orcus is here. The bearded giant of a nemesis is the last person that I want near Vicky and her friend. In an instant, I transport myself up into their room. It's empty.

"Shit." I pull out my mobile and dial my father. "The girl has gone missing. Orcus is around."

"I'll send reinforcements," he replies, and I hear chairs scraping in the background. My backup is on its way.

"I'll start looking."

"Stay safe."

I don't reply but hang up my phone and put it back in my pocket. I shut my eyes and allow the heightened senses, which all gods have, to work. The sound of a body being dragged down the hallway on the floor below has me running from the room and down the stairs, two at a time.

"Orcus," I shout when I see the darkly clothed figure. He looks up at me, and a twisted smirk crosses his face—he holds Susan. Beside him, holding an unconscious Vicky is the accused man from my court case a few days ago.

"Too late, Mars," Orcus growls. He's always been more ogre than man. His job is to punish the broken oaths that people make—he takes it very seriously and disciplines them by eating the flesh warm from their bodies. Shame, he only chooses to enact his judgment on those who don't deserve it. I step forward and plant myself firmly, ready to attack. My hand shoots out and my spear appears.

"No, I'm fashionably on time." I point my magical weapon at them. "Leave now."

"Don't worry, I plan on it."

"Without the girls," I add and send a lightning bolt to the feet of the twisted human man who holds the woman I need to protect.

"Oh." Orcus shrugs. I'm sure that he has drool dripping over his chin. He's a disgusting creature, and one that I'd be more than happy to put down. "But I was hoping to take the girls with me. We wanted to have some fun." The obvious sarcasm in his tone isn't lost on me.

"Not going to happen." I humor him. "These girls aren't the sort who would enjoy the type of fun you have in mind. You know that my father has additional people on the way, right now, so just leave."

"Your father's a right pain. Always interfering where he isn't wanted. Nobody put him in charge, you know."

"I think the fact that he's the King of God's means he's in charge. Now, do as I say or feel the wrath of war."

Orcus throws his head back and laughs. The man standing next to him looks up at the booming sound.

"I'm not sure you should laugh about war." He gulps at his partner.

"Why?" Orcus replies. "War went soft ages ago. You think the torment in the world nowadays is anything like the wars we used to have. The ones he started with his anger. I remember men being ripped apart, bodies lying all over the land. Loved ones crying endlessly for the suffering and starvation they felt. Mars has gone weak. You've become too much like the man behind the desk you portray. A ruthless lawyer, your only power is in court, now. We hold the power out here."

I breathe deeply to try and remain calm, but the harsher side of the god I am has been pricked. He wants blood, retribution for the slur on his name. I hear shouts of a battle in my head–a war fought in the lands of deserts and religious strife. It intensifies, my emotions battling with my need to tamper them down. Bombs explode, gunshots ring out, cries of victory and defeat resonate around the walls of the rundown hotel. Red mist descends over my vision. I charge at Orcus, but he vanishes into thin air, taking Susan with him.

"Orcus." The vile creature that tortures women shouts after him.

"Let her go," I snarl and snap. He pushes Vicky toward me, and she lands with a thump on the floor. I step over her so that my feet are either side of her. She's protected between my legs–nobody can harm her without going through me first.

"The courts may have found you innocent, but I know what you did. I saw the evidence. You killed humans and goddesses. Do you know that they're reincarnated but have memories of what happened in their previous lives? They'll always remember what you did to them. They may not see your face, but they'll remember the pain, the suffering, they felt and how they longed for death to escape your clutches. I think it's about time that you know exactly what they felt." I point my spear at him, and the skin on the left side of his face peels from the temple down to his chin. It hangs there, swinging. He screams; I rejoice. The muscle underneath vibrates with movement, and his crimson life force starts to drip to the marble floor like tears.

"You feel it, yet?" I rasp, the war in my head is getting louder and louder. I point the spear again. This time the flesh on his arm starts to blister like it is burning. The acrid smell of incinerated flesh floods my nostrils.

"Mars," Orcus calls behind me, and I spin around and send a flash of energy from my spear toward him. It misses and hits the wall behind him when he disappears and then reappears next to the man who I've been torturing. "We'll be back for her." He retorts, and they both leave. The corridor goes silent except for the conflicts that rage on in my head. My emotions have never been so closely linked to the world as they are now."

A feminine moan has me looking down to my feet. Vicky's eyes flutter, and she opens them slowly. They shut involuntarily again before springing open.

"Mars," she breathlessly utters and grabs my leg. It's my turn to lose my breath; it hitches, and I gulp for air. Her compassion, love, and beauty floods through me from the skin to skin contact. My mind quietens, hushed weeping is all I hear. No sounds of battle rage, fires are extinguished, guns empty. The war inside me is defeated for now. "What's happening? Where's Susan." She looks around the hallway.

"How did I get here?" She looks back up at me, again. Her eyes are wide open, and she's terrified. They flick to my right and the massive spear that I still hold in my hand. "And what the fuck is that?"

VENUS
Chapter six

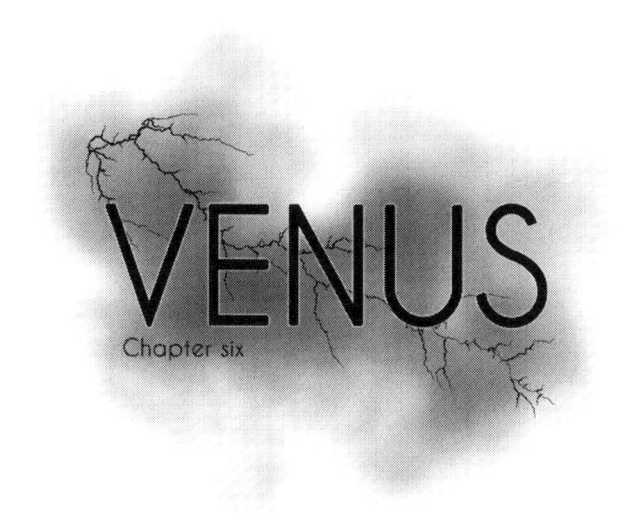

Memories wash over me. Drugged. There had been something in the champagne.

Mars stares down at me, a fearsome sight, a spear clutched mercilessly in one hand. He looks practically heathen. Savage. Dark eyes burn with a wealth of emotion. He's a terrifying form. Again, the power he wields overwhelms me. It smothers me.

I've never felt so vulnerable. So exposed.

Sobs rise in my throat, I scoot backward on my ass trying to escape.

"Vicky, it's ok."

I don't believe him. How can I trust him now? He's probably the one who knocked us out. Some pervert trying to kidnap us for god knows what.

"What have you done with Susan?" The tremor in my voice betrays my emotions.

"I'm not the one who…" Glancing at the weapon he's

holding, he grimaces. In a flash, it's gone as if it never even existed.

"No. No. No." Twisting onto my hands and knees, I crawl away faster, the coarse carpet rough against my palms. "This isn't happening."

Footsteps follow. "Vicky, calm down."

"Get the fuck away from me."

"Bella, just let me explain."

He's fucking nuts. I need to contact the police. Whatever he's done with my friend, I won't let him get away with it. Moving faster, I manage to stumble up using my knees onto my feet. Even before I manage to make it to the stairwell, a strong arm snags me around the waist.

My scream echoes down the corridor.

One second we're in the hotel, the next I find myself in a spacious, modern living room.

Screaming again, I start to struggle. This has to be a hallucination, an effect from whatever was in our drinks. Maybe I'm dreaming?

Mars keeps my back pinned to his hard-muscled front.

Fingernails digging into the tanned flesh of his forearm, I claw deeply, trying to budge the prison.

Mars hisses. "So, we do this the hard way."

The fingers of his free hand tangle in my hair, and my head is forced painfully back.

Tears spring to my eyes as I yelp.

Compelling me to move until, the solid surface of a table meets the tops of my thighs, and then bending me over, he pins me with ease.

Reaching back, I slap at anything I can connect with. It's a mistake. I'm desperate. Fear blinds me to anything but the urge to escape.

Taking my wrists in a bruising grip, he keeps them clasped behind my back.

"Get the fuck off me." Bucking, kicking, I soon realize it's useless. He has me exactly where he wants me. At his mercy and unable to move.

Mars' length dominates my smaller frame. As sanity returns, I become aware of the blatant press of his rigid cock, which remains in his trousers, against my lower spine.

"Now, are you going to calm down?" His voice is a deep murmur by my ear.

"What are you? An Alien trying to kidnap us for experimentation?"

His chuckle sends heat over my skin. "You really have a vivid imagination, don't you?"

"After what I just saw, what the hell am I supposed to believe?"

The hand still wrapped in my hair flexes; his fingertips start to massage my scalp.

A moan trickles from my lips at the tingling sensation. Shoulders slumping, the fight drains from my body.

The more we remain in this position, the harder it is to ignore the stirring of arousal awakening inside me.

Lips brush the back of my neck. A whispering butterfly press of his mouth. My head drops forward, it's instinctual, allowing him more access. An animal impulse I can't ignore.

"Your so beautiful, Vicky. I've wanted you from the first moment I saw you." Mars confesses, his exploration moving to my shoulder.

A sharp nip of teeth makes me shudder with need.

There's no denying I want him to. The more he touches me, the wetter I become. I don't understand it. His effect. This feeling he invokes. Yet, no matter how I try, I can't deny it. He's a liar. A kidnapper. Probably some kind of pervert. I shouldn't be so horny.

Gyrating his hips, he grinds his cock into my ass. "Tell me you want me too."

Thought evaporates. Every wrong or right. Fear. Susan. They vanish as lust roars up so fiercely my head spins.

"Yes." It's a breathy whisper. I can't deny it. It's uttered with a longing I can't hide.

The grip on my wrists eases. Hauling me around, he sandwiches me between his hard-packed body and the table.

Lips find mine. They plunder and ravage. Tongue tracing the seam of my mouth, asking for entry.

Without a care, I allow him access.

Mars groans in his throat as he deepens the kiss. Hand cradling the back of my skull, he takes charge. It's brutal, raw, yet, I crave it. Sweeping me away, I'm lost in only the taste and smell of this dominant masculine male.

"I need you," his words are muttered when he breaks apart. I can hear the desperation.

I want him too. Need him to fuck me. Everything inside me screams for something I know I shouldn't want. I'm so turned on common sense is no longer a factor.

Clasping my hips, he lifts me easily, and sits me on the table. I don't protest. With eager hands, I help him gather my skirt, dragging it high up to my waist.

Hands shaking, he unbuckles his pants. His cock springs free, bobbing in my direction. It's beautiful, long, and thick, and for a second, I feel panic I might not be able to take him all.

"Relax." Cupping my chin, he kisses me breathless. "We'll fit perfectly, I promise."

"Please...please fuck me," I keen. All I want is what he can give me. No more words just him filling me.

Pushing my panties aside, he slides the crown of his cock across my wet folds, coating it in my juices.

Its heat makes me moan. Arching forward, he drives me insane with the teasing friction.

Parting me legs further, I bear myself for his possession. I'll beg if he makes me. It's insane, but I have no control.

Mars' face lights with triumph. Flashing me a sexy smile, he pushes home in one long, single thrust.

A groan bursts from my lips. His thickness claiming me in such a way I feel it all the way to my soul.

"Sweetheart, your pussy is so tight." His hands find my hips for better purchase.

Legs wrapping around his lean waist, all I can do is cling to him as he begins to take me. Hard, wild, in a way I've never experienced before. It buzzes through my nerve endings, sending pleasure swirling through my blood.

"Mars," I say his name in awe.

Grunting in response, he thrusts into me harder, faster as if somehow, he's attempting to merge us as one. Joining his rhythm, I lose myself in our mutual need. A desire to reach the pinnacle we're both racing to, to topple over together.

I find mine first. Limbs stiffening, head thrown back, an orgasm rolls through me so fiercely I see stars. Mars follows closely behind. My inner walls squeezing his cock in the aftermath; I feel it pulse right before hot ribbons of cum fill me.

Panting, shaking, forehead resting in the crook of his neck, pleasure wraps me in a daze of bliss.

MARS

Chapter seven

I think I might have just had an out of body experience. Sex has always been great for me. I mean what could possibly be wrong with sticking your dick into a warm and willing hole? Some experiences are better than others. I mean the hole has to be just the right level of wetness and can't be so loose that my dick falls out every time I get it to the tip. No, I definitely need a tight hole. I'm not fussy whether it's mouth, asshole, or pussy either. I'll stick my dick anywhere, but Vicky–*holy shit*–I think my head may have exploded. I know my dick certainly did. It's still pulsating and leaking cum even though I've had her tucked into the crook of my arm for about half and hour now. Actually, no, scrap that, it's getting hard again and ready for round two.

"Susan." Vicky sits bolt upright, and my dick shrinks inside itself knowing that round two is unlikely to happen. She turns to me with a look of worry on her face that has my normally dead heart beating rapidly. "Where is she?" She scrambles from the table. "I have to find her, and then I'm coming back here, so you can explain to me what the fuck is going on? I mean, we just appeared in what I assume is your house. That doesn't normally happen. Not unless I'm so drunk I've no idea how I got home from a club when I wake the next morning, puking my guts up." She pulls her t-shirt over her breasts, and I lament the loss of those perky nipples. Her skirt covers up her curvy ass, and I almost want to cry. What the hell is happening to me? I'm not a sap like this. I fucked her. She can leave, right; we've done the horizontal mambo. Love them and leave them. Except, fuck, Orcus has her best mate and will, at this very moment, probably be trying to torment the goddess out of her. They'll soon discover they have the wrong girl, though.

"Vicky, I can't let you leave here." Common-sense overrules my dick–the latter sulks.

"You can't let me leave?" She places her hands on her hips and stares me down. "So, I was right. You are some kind of freak who gets his kicks from kidnapping people. Oh, my god. I slept with you. I must have gone insane." She freezes and then jiggles as if she's feeling something unpleasant running down her leg. "We didn't use a condom! You better not have any diseases. I'm such an idiot. I'm leaving." She stomps to the door. I shut my eyes, dematerialize, leaving the sex tangled sheets behind and reappear naked in her path.

She screams. I slap my hand over her mouth and hold a finger up, compelling her to listen to me. Her bright blue eyes go wide open with terror.

"No, we did it the hard way already. You have far too much energy for someone I've just fucked. Sit on the sofa." Her head shakes, and then her teeth bite down into my hand.

Mother fucking.........

"Enough!" I shout. "I've got people already out looking

for Susan. There's nothing you can do. You're safe here. Out there, they'll come for you. Now, I'm going to remove my hand. No more screaming. I don't have close neighbors, but I don't think now is the time to alert the people I do have in the house to your being here. Not when you're covered in my cum, and I'm butt naked as the day I was born."

I pause and allow her a minute to digest everything I've said. She eventually nods at me, indicating she won't scream, so I remove my hand.

"What are you?" Her voice trembles as she speaks.

"Sit down." She staggers back to the sofa on wobbly legs. I go to my bedroom knowing I can be back in an instant if she tries to leave. I grab a pair of track pants and pull them on. My dick flopping about while having this conversation isn't going to work well. I rub at my temples; the sounds of battle that were silenced are slowly starting to return. I go back to the lounge, and I find Vicky sitting silently on the sofa and staring out at the view of Rome.

"Where is my friend?" she stutters.

I take a seat opposite her on a Queen Anne chair, which takes pride of place in my room, which is decorated to my masculine tastes. The floors are marble with black rugs. The massive sofa and a matching television dominate the room. The rest of the furniture is sparse, a set of drawers, which are mainly empty, and a table on one of the rugs. It's all highly fashionable brands of décor, but to me, it's a place I try to rest. However, with Vicky in the center of my sofa, it's transformed into something entirely different. She adds the feminine touch. Bringing my right leg up, I settle it on my left knee.

"Your friend has been taken by a man called Orcus and

his henchman, a man I was trying to get imprisoned, recently. Unfortunately, he was cleared of all charges."

"What were the charges?" She knits her hands together in her lap, the top one stroking the bottom in comfort.

"Rape, murder, flaying."

She gasps and brings her hands to her mouth as if to stem the feeling of sickness I know she must be feeling. Reading the court files during the case, I felt it myself.

"We have to call the police."

I shake my head.

"Why not?" she pleads.

"There's nothing they can do to help. This is beyond their remit."

"Because of the fact that you are so obviously not human."

"Yes," I reply and fiddle with a lost strand on my pants.

"This Orcus and the other guy, they're like you?"

"Orcus is. The man with the poor career choices is human."

A tear drops from her eyes and tumbles down her cheek.

"I don't understand. Why us? Are they trying to get back at you or something? Did they target us because we were walked back to the hotel by you?"

"No." I look her direct in the eye. "It's because you're the same as me."

She bursts out laughing. It wasn't really the reaction I was expecting

"I don't think so? I'm Vicky Valentine, a twenty-five-year-old from Devon. I'm a nobody. I'm nothing like you."

I lean forward and rub my hand against my head. I can see why my father advised that it would be better to get to know this woman first before telling her who she was. I'm not cut out for this. I'd be better off searching for Susan.

I'm the God of War, not the God of 'Talking about it'. Maybe I could summon Bellona and ask her to do it. No, the room smells of sex. The Goddess of War would castrate me for dropping my trousers at the first opportunity. I've the strangest feeling that Vicky wouldn't be impressed either.

"You aren't, Vicky. You aren't twenty-five, and you're not from Devon."

"I think I must still be under the influence of whatever drug they gave me. No, no…..I got really bad sunburn sitting out all day, and I'm hallucinating. That's it. I'll wake up in a minute, and I'll be curled up in my bed."

"Not going to happen," I retort.

"Oh, shut up, you're a bad dream." She waves her hand in my direction to dismiss me.

"Feel between your thighs, Vicky. My cum's dripping down them. My cock has been so deep inside your pussy that it will still be throbbing. This is real." I watch as she shifts in her seat, testing my theory.

"Who am I?"

"For certain, I don't know. I suspect, but I won't know for certain until you face the trials to reveal your true nature."

"Trials?"

"Something we all have to go through."

"My head hurts."

I want to go to her and comfort her, but it's the wrong thing. Every time I touch her, I lose myself in her true nature. My god senses it even if she can't, yet.

"It's a lot to take in. You're not the first and won't be the last. There are so many of us missing.

"So, what happened? Did we crash from space or something?"

She still thinks we're aliens. I snort a little laugh, and she glares at me.

"This maybe funny to you, but it isn't to me. I'm terrified."

"I know. Look, we aren't aliens. In fact, we were here long before the humans."

"Long before the humans! Just how old are you?"

"Roughly four-billion-years-old. I'm not exactly sure of my birthdate. My parents didn't really keep records."

"Four billion!" Her mouth fell open, and she gawped at me. "How old am I?"

"Roughly the same," I reply with trepidation.

"Damn, I've aged well."

"I thought you said this wasn't a laughing matter?" I question only to be greeted with an evil glare.

"I can make jokes. You can't."

"Noted."

"So, we're four billion years old. What does that make us? The first people on Earth."

"Gods." My reply is blunter than I mean it be.

"Gods," she repeats with sarcasm lacing her tone.

"Yes. What do you know about Roman Mythology?"

"Mars." A moment of clarification flashes over her face, and she pales even further. "You're the God of War?"

"Yes. The one and only."

"But aren't you evil? I mean in that Wonder Woman film, I watched a few months back, you wanted to kill everyone."

The urge I get to kill, every so often, resurfaces at that comment. I'm never portrayed that well in modern history. That's one thing that went wrong with the humans when they first discovered us. They made up so many stories about us. Just because I'm the God of War doesn't mean I advocate it. I spend more of my time trying to prevent the idiot humans from trying to kill each other than declaring invasions on different countries. And don't even get me started on the number of children I'm supposed to have had. As far as I know, there are *none*. I wrap myself, well normally, but I think we'll discuss that at a different time.

"My role is to try and prevent war, not create it."

"You had a few slip up over the years, then."

"One or two...thousand. I'm amazed humans ever get on with their penchant for destruction."

"Who do you think I am?" She sits forward on the sofa. Her arms rest on her lissome legs.

"I can't tell you. It's something you need to discover yourself."

"Right"–she rolls her eyes– "you know, if you hadn't made that spear thing disappear and me move through space, I wouldn't believe a word coming out of your mouth, right now."

"It's a lot to take in."

"So, your father, he's like the God of Gods, isn't he? What's his name? Zeus?"

"Zeus is Greek Mythology. My father is Jupiter, and yes, he's the King of Gods. He's also the owner of our law firm."

"So, the Roman gods are lawyers in Rome. I think I need a drink."

I get to my feet and go over to a cupboard that contains a decanter of rich red wine. I pour her a glass, hand it to her. I take a seat on the sofa this time. She downs the glass in one.

"It's good."

"Should be. It's a recipe given to me by Julius Caesar himself. I have vineyards up in Tuscany, making it to his exact specifications."

"Julius Caesar."

"Yes."

I await a witty response from her, but this time, she burst into tears.

"I'm scared."

I scoot forward on the chair and bring her into my arms.

"You'll remember soon. It's a lot to take in."

"I need to put it aside, for now." She breathes in deeply. "I need to focus on Susan."

A knock at the door interrupts us.

"Enter!" I shout. My brother, Apollo, comes in. He looks defeated, and I know instantly the news I'm about to deliver to this woman who is slowly entwining herself around my heart. I wave him away.

"Who was that?"

"Apollo."

"The God of Music?"

"Amongst other things."

"He didn't say anything?"

"He didn't need to. It was written all over his face."

"What was?"

I take a deep breath.

"I'm sorry. They didn't reach Susan in time. She's dead."

VENUS
Chapter eight

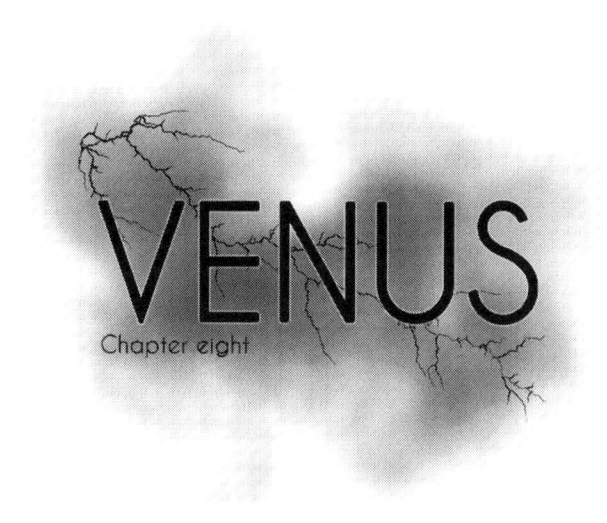

Susan is dead. Mars' words ring through my head. The wail of denial is ripped from my chest to escape through my lips. Shaking my head, I curl my hands into fists. This was supposed to be fun. Me and my best friend forever. A trip of a lifetime. Not a fucking nightmare. I feel like I've fallen down a fucked-up rabbit hole.

"No...no, you're lying!" My clumsy attempt to strike him is quickly disarmed.

Hand manacling my wrists, he draws them against his hard-muscled pecs at the same time, snuggling me closer into his comforting embrace.

I don't want his comfort. It's his fault I'm here. Whatever weird shit I'm mixed up in, none of this happened before we met him.

"I'm so sorry, Vicky." His softly spoken words are sorrowful.

My tears fall faster, and my shoulders are shaking. I can't

stop the torrent that's been unleashed. "Sh..she can't be..be dead."

Mars rocks me gently but doesn't say another word.

Pressing my face into the warm flesh of his chest, I let my misery runs its course. I don't know how long we sit there. By the time I'm done, my exhaustion is heavy. As awareness returns, I find myself snuggled on his lap; his larger body is my haven.

"Bring her back." Voice hoarse, my tired gaze flicks up to his face. "If you're a god...if we're gods, we can bring her back."

Sad brown eyes meet mine. "That's not how it works."

"Bullshit."

A long sigh escapes him. "Only certain gods have power over death, and neither you nor I are one of them."

"Then find one who does."

"Vicky, trust me, you wouldn't want to meet the one who does."

"Why?" I ask, pulling myself free of his embrace. Slipping off his lap, I stand on unsteady legs. I'm abruptly aware of the smell of sex in the room. His cum still oozing down my thighs and sticky in my panties from where we fucked on his table.

"Because he's the one who was hunting you." Mars informs me. Although he remains relaxed, I sense he's poised to catch me if I fall.

"No one was after me until I met you," I accuse, eyes narrowing with my rising anger. "My life was normal. Susan...Susan was alive."

A shadow of emotion I can't identify passes over Mars' face, sending a nerve ticking in his tightening jaw. "You were on their radar before we even met."

"If I can't bring my friend back, then I don't want to be like you."

"Bella, you don't have a choice. Now that we've met, things have been set in motion. You'll remember, and your powers will return."

That knowledge terrifies me. Will I still be me or someone else? Is what he's telling me true? Am I an ancient goddess? The idea is absurd, but I can't discount what I've seen with my own eyes. A dull ache pulses through my forehead, signaling an oncoming migraine.

"I need to use your bathroom and clean myself up."

A frown crinkles his brow at my change of direction and my clipped tone. "Of course. I'll show you where it is. Take your time."

Closing my eyes for a second, I wince as pain lances behind my right eye.

"Are you alright?" Mars asks in concern.

Absently, I massage at the spot, trying to rub away the discomfort. "Headache."

"There are painkillers in the bathroom cabinet."

I sense him, moving closer. A tingle of air sends goosebumps over my skin. Eyes popping open, I take an instinctive step back.

His expression darkens, and he regards me with a brooding look. "You don't have to be frightened of me, Vicky. I'm not going to hurt you."

Crossing my arms under my breasts, I refuse to meet his eyes. "I'm not."

Mars doesn't move. The heat of his gaze on my face makes me blush, but I don't look up to meet it.

"I'll show you the bathroom and get you those

painkillers," he finally says after it feels like an eternity has passed.

Following him from the room, I glance around the bedroom we enter. It's huge. Decorated in dark blues and black, every inch of it screams masculinity. It lacks a woman's touch.

Mars directs me toward a door. Pushing it open, he shows me into a luxurious en-suite.

"Tablets are here. You just need to take two." Moving to a cabinet, he efficiently retrieves a packet. "I keep them for guests as I don't use them myself." He hesitates but doesn't continue.

I'm thankful he doesn't. I've taken as much as I can, right now, and maybe he realizes anymore, and I might break.

Arms still wrapped around my middle, I watch as he places the foiled packet next to the sink.

"Towels are on the shelf. Use whatever you like."

I don't answer. Instead, I wait patiently for him to leave.

The second the door clicks closed behind him, I let my shoulders sag. Thinking is almost impossible with the growing headache. Plodding to the sink, I free two pills and swallow them down. Relief can't come soon enough. With the pounding in my skull increasing, it feels like my head might explode. I don't bother to check for a lock on the door. With Mars being able to magically appear and reappear, there's no point.

Finding a large towel, I leave it out on a nearby chair. The process of undressing is slow and shaky. I'm so drained everything becomes an effort.

The hot water does little to revive my senses. I'm lost in a fog. A haze that's enveloped my grief-stricken mind.

It's enough, though, to scrub myself clean. Wipe away

Mars' scent and the evidence of our coupling. I still can't believe we had unprotected sex. I've never been so stupid in my life. Always been so careful.

Slipping from the shower, the towel is soft and comforting as I dry every inch of my skin. Exhaustion hits me again, harder this time. I don't try to fight it. Maybe it's still the effects of the drugs or the emotional turmoil. All I know is I need to sleep.

Spying a robe on the back of the door, I unhook it. It swamps me as I drag it on. The material feels expensive, and Mars' smell lingers on the fabric.

Padding out into the bedroom, I find it empty. Guess he's decided to give me space after all.

Voices murmur, muffled from the other side of the door, which has been left ajar. Straying closer, I listen.

"How is she?"

"Scared, confused, which isn't surprising, really." Mars replies to the stranger's voice.

"I don't think fucking her so soon helped things."

A strained pause follows. "She draws me like no other female ever has. It hasn't been easy to control myself around her, and I…"

"Slipped up." The other male finishes on a sigh. "You're supposed to gain her trust not complicate things further."

"I think things are beyond complicated right now, no matter what I've done."

"You've got that right. Keep her here at all costs; we can't afford to lose this one."

The distinct sound of glass clinking reverberates. Are they having a drink? Adding ice maybe?

Quietly as I can, I close the door, deciding at the last second to lock it. It might not stop Mars, but it will keep any human intruders out, which brings me a small measure of comfort.

Dragging my feet toward the bed, the soft mattress catches me when I drop. Lethargy has a hold over me that not even I can shake. Curling onto the bed, I let it cradle me. Before I'm settled, my eyes droop closed.

"Vicky."

"Susan? You're alive!" Blinking in confusion, I glance around the strange room. What happened to the bedroom? How the hell did I get here?

Rough rock makes up the walls. Uneven, crude, it's like someone has chiseled them into life. Stark white bones gleam from their positions around the room. It looks ritualistic.

"Vicky, please, you have to help me." My friend's voice is pleading. Pain resonates in her words along with her terror.

Barefoot, I creep over the smooth, fine sand, which makes up the floor. "Where are you? Why can't I see you?"

She's nowhere in sight. Light dances across the strange walls from the flaming torches hanging on metal brackets. It's odd. Medieval. As if I've taken a step back in time. Without windows, I have no way to tell where I am. Yet, it feels as if I'm underground. Somewhere deep and hidden.

"I don't have time to explain. This is a dream, but I'm communicating to you through it. There's a church, Santa Maria della Concezione dei Cappuccini, I'm there. Please hurry. I don't know how long I have until they come back."

I know the place she means. A church famous for its crypt of human skeletal remains believed to be those of Capuchin friars who'd been buried there. One of the places we were supposed to visit.

"Stay where you are." I tell her, urgently, turning in a circle yet still not locating her. "Mars can help us."

A sob follows my words. "No... don't...he's one of the men who took me. They want to hurt me. They have already. He...he told me I was special. A goddess...then he raped me and tortured me..."

My heart twists. I trusted him. How stupid he must think I am. I'd been dumb enough to believe his story that Susan was dead. That he was saving me from some great evil. This has to be a sick game to him. What he did to my friend he probably has the same planned for me. After all, what do I really know about him apart from he's the God of War? He could be just feeding me lies.

"He'll hurt you too, Vicky." She continues desperately. "Oh god, the things he did to me. Don't be blinded by the pull he has. A feeling of connection. It's a trick to reel you in."

I can't abandon her. Won't. Not now I know she's still alive, and I can save her.

"I'm going to get you out." I tell her; my voice strong with resolve. "Hide if you can and wait for me. I'll get to you as soon as I can."

Susan doesn't answer.

The subterranean room melts away in a growing fog of swirling white.

MARS
Chapter nine

The wine sticks in my throat. I don't want to be sitting here with my brothers and father drinking and making plans. I want to be in my bedroom with Vicky, holding her to ensure that she's ok. In the space of a few hours, she's had so much to take in, and I know that she's falling apart. She may not have come into her powers, but the confusion and anguish surging through her body is felt deeply in the pores of mine.

"Mars?" my father speaks, and I'm drawn out of my reflection, "What do you think about getting Vicky out of Rome, maybe take her Tuscany."

"Until she's seen her friend's body, I doubt that she'll want to go anywhere."

My brother Apollo shifts uncomfortably in his seat.

"I'm not sure that's a good idea. They messed her up pretty badly."

"Something tells me I won't have the option to stop her."

My father chuckles.

"She's definitely Venus; I remember her being so stubborn."

"I'll talk to her in the morning. Look, I don't mean to be rude, but I think I should go and check on her."

Hercules and Apollo look at each other, and their mouths drop open. My father just sits back in his chair with a contented look.

"It's happening," he states.

"What?" I ask.

"The joining of two gods. It's such a special thing. I thought it was just you showing off your virility, as usual, and disobeying my rules about getting to know her as a friend, not a lover, but no, I see now that you didn't have a choice. She really is calling to you."

"It's strong." My answer is blunt. "Nobody's ever held this amount of power over me before. She silences the war with only a touch."

"That's because she's your equal, my son, go with it."

Hercules and Apollo both laugh.

"The great lover's going to be off the market. Might mean that we get first choice of the women for once," Hercules states, flexing his arm muscles.

"Not if you go around doing that you won't." I roll my eyes and place the wine down on the table.

My father stands and walks toward the door.

"Apollo, Hercules, come. We have things we need to be working on. Hercules, see what you can do to make Vicky's friend more suitable for inspection."

"What?" Hercules moans, "Really? I hate that job."

"It's your turn so stop complaining." My father leaves, and my brothers follow with Hercules still complaining. I pick up the glasses and walk them to the kitchen sink where I run them under the tap to clean them before putting them on the draining board to dry. I've always been a little bit of a neat freak. I guess when you hear chaos on a daily basis you need some normality and order in your world. The ever-present headache that I've had for the last few days has returned, and I rub at my temples to try to dispel the pain. The voices are loud, tonight. I've been trying to focus on Vicky sleeping in my bed, but they keep interrupting the silence of her slumber. I'd heard her turn the lock. She knows that it won't keep me from entering the room, but still, she did it. Was it because of her lingering doubts as to my part in all of this, or her sheer terror resulting from the death of her friend and the knowledge she's a god? Mind reading is one power that I'd really like to have, but unfortunately, it escapes me.

I flick the light switches to turn them off and stride purposefully toward the bedroom. My path is blocked, though, when Bellona materializes.

"I've just spoken to your father." I look her up and down. She's dressed in only a lightweight robe. "He told me what happened."

Without thinking about it, I allow her to lead me to the sofa. She takes a seat next to me and perches on her knees. I'm still topless, having not bothered to dress properly when it became obvious to my father what Vicky and I had done. Bellona uses her hand to massage my shoulders. I know I'm full of tension and relax back into the softness of her caress.

"You shouldn't be here," I finally speak.

"How can I not, when I know that you are suffering?"

"You aren't my official consort, Bellona. Just the woman I go to when I need no strings attached sex."

She halts her ministrations to my shoulder and then resumes with the pressure of the massage increasing.

"I'm the one you come to when you need release from the stresses of your day."

"I've had my release today, thank you."

She turns her head toward my bedroom. I know that she finally feels Vicky's presence in my bed.

"Does your father know?"

"Yes," I reply curtly.

"That's not a method I've seen your men employ before. Fuck the goddess before she even knows she is one."

"You have no reason to be jealous." I pull my shoulder away from her hands. "And you shouldn't be here. Go home."

"Fuck me, Mars. You need another release, and only the type I can give you."

"Go home." I get to my feet, uncaring that I knock into her, and that, losing her balance in her precarious position, she tumbles to the floor. She starts laughing. I glare down at her, wanting her gone from my house. The voices in my head are masking over Vicky all the time now, and I need to check that she's alright.

"She'll never give you what I can; you know that as well as I do."

"No," I spit at her. "She can give me something so much better. A goddess that hasn't whored herself out to most of my family."

She gets to her feet in an instant and slaps me hard across the face.

"Is that anyway to talk to the mother of your child?"

It's my turn to laugh.

"Enyalius could be anyone's son."

"He's yours." She shouts back at me. "I slept with nobody else during that time, but you."

I turn my back to her. I know in my heart that Enyalius,

or Luigi as I call him for a more modern name, is my son. You only have to look at him to know that. The spirit and aptitude he shows toward preventing war is already there. It's hardly surprising when both his parents are the divinities of it. I take a deep breath to calm myself down.

"I'm sorry, Bellona. I'm tired. It's been a long day. I have to look after Vicky. If she's Venus, then she's an important god for us to have found. We can't risk her falling into Pluto's hands."

I hold my hand out to the woman who for a long time I've sought comfort in. But at this very moment, I realize it's only ever been physical, and the emotional side of love just isn't there for me. She takes it and pulls herself back up to her feet.

"Do you think she's Venus?"

"I do."

Bellona silences and looks at the floor.

"War and beauty combined."

"Yes."

"I wonder if we'll ever find a male version. A god of love."

Her reply is sad. I know the pain that Bellona has going on in her head daily. It's the same as mine. She's tried to fill it with love in the wrong places, though. Sexual love isn't always the same as love of the heart. That's what Vicky will give, if she's Venus.

"I'm afraid I don't think he'll exist. Only the female of our species is capable of the beauty and love that's needed for that position. In men, there's always a darkness, a selfishness if you like. We don't have the capability to have the complete innocence needed for the Goddess of Love."

"I don't think either of us have ever had the innocence you speak of–it's too ingrained in our natures to fight."

"And it's what we'll always do with complete class."

She lets out a little laugh before immediately placing her hand over her mouth so as not to give me an inch in this war that always rages between us.

"I should get back to Louis." She looks toward my bedroom door again – her face is full of regret. "This will be goodbye, won't it?"

"It'll never be goodbye, Bellona. We share something special in Louis. He binds us together forever. But physically, yes, that ends now." She nods her acceptance, even if it's with reluctance. "I tell you what, when this is over, why don't I come and stay for a few days with you as a friend and the father of your son. We can spend time with him together. He's the one we must put our love into now."

"I'd like that." She stands up on her tiptoes and presses a kiss to my cheek. I allow it because it's symbolic of friendship, not the sexual affection that we once shared for each other. "Be careful, Pluto is getting stronger and stronger. I don't know how much longer we'll be able to keep him down."

"I will." She turns and vanishes into thin air. I do the same and rematerialize in my bedroom. I look toward the bed, and my whole-body strains with anguish. There where I expect Vicky is nothing but a card. When I step closer, I get the confirmation I fear; it's Pluto's business card.

VENUS

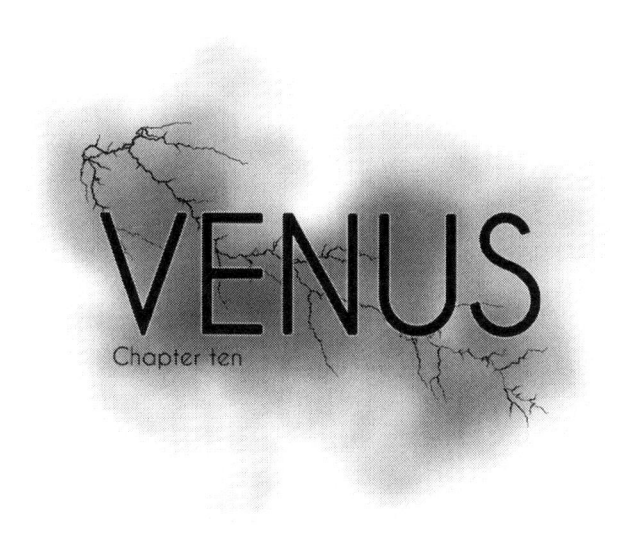

Chapter ten

Pain thunders through my skull as a groan leaves my lips. Eyelids fluttering open, I stare up at the stark stone ceiling. The last thing I remember is being outside the church. How I got from Mars' bedroom to there, I don't remember. I just know the need to be there was overwhelming.

Susan! I'd heard her. She'd called to me from just inside the church. The pain. Oh my god, the pain in her voice had been heartbreaking. Brow furrowing, I try to recall more. Once I'd stepped inside, there's nothing but a blank.

Goosebumps racing over my skin, I'm suddenly aware I'm naked. A lumpy mattress is against my back. Panicked, I move to sit up.

Hard, unmoving metal manacles on my wrists and ankles are shackled to a bed frame, preventing my attempt to cover myself.

"Awake at last."

Turning my head, I find the owner of the voice, standing

watching me. Shoulder leaning against the door jam, I recognize him immediately. The waiter from the hotel. His beady, dark eyes run over me. Wiry torso, bare, grubby stained jeans hang low on his hips.

"Where's Susan? Where's my friend?"

My burst of anger is met with a smile. "Didn't your new boyfriend tell you? She's dead."

No. I shake my head in denial. "She's here."

"Ah yes, the dream. My Master enjoyed that." He chuckles. "Thought it would lure you out."

A trap. Turning my face away from his smug expression, a sob rises in my throat. Hope withers and dies. My heart shattering even more than it already has tonight.

"Oh, don't worry," my captor continues softly. "I'll treat you just as nice as I did your friend. How do you think Mars will react to that? Have you bonded with him already? Maybe he'll feel your pain. I hope so."

Footsteps draw my attention back. Stalking towards me with purpose, he begins to unbuckle his belt. Eyes widening, panic chokes me. Twisting in my chains, I try futilely to escape. Dragging it free, he weighs the heaviness of it in his other hand. "You have such lovely skin. I can't wait to mess it up."

The strike comes with no warning. Hard, fast, the bite of the leather sears across my abdomen. A scream rips from my throat. Even before it's finished, another one rises as more lashes rain down on my helpless body. It burns. Everywhere he whips pulses with agony.

He shows me no mercy. Blow after blow growing in frenzied intensity. This monster is determined to break my body. Something wet and warm trails down my hip. The metallic smell of blood reaches my nose. I can taste it in my mouth. Wounds sting open and bleed, inflicted by the metal buckle of his belt.

"Scream louder," he instructs, voice ragged with excitement. "Don't hold back. No one will hear you down here. The others learned that quickly…. so did Susan."

Jerking my face away, the instrument of my torture narrowly misses my face. The lash licks instead over my bare shoulder and up my neck.

"Please," I beg. "Please, stop it hurts…why are you hurting me?" Tears shimmer before my eyes. Already racing down my face, their dampness spreads across my trembling cheeks.

The man laughs. "Because I like it. Because I can."

Flinching at the pleasure in his voice, I wait rigidly for the next strike. It takes a second for the sound of material being shed to register.

No. The one word screams out inside me. He's going to rape me. Discarding the belt, he takes his cock in one hand. Veiny, thick, the end is purple and bulbous. Working his length, he begins to jerk off. All the while, his greedy eyes running over me and the damage he's caused.

"Oh yeah, baby, look at you now. You're going to bruise up so lovely." He pants. "You'll be the perfect canvas." His hand moves faster as he grows harder, his cock swelling with his lust. Groaning, hips pumping forward, his excitements reaches its climax. Hot ribbons of cum coat my stomach. Scalding, his seed burns my throbbing open flesh. Sobs wrack my agonized body. I wish I could curl up into a protective ball. Wake up in bed and find this is all a nightmare. A hand touches my cum stained stomach, making be cringe. Through tear stained eyes, I see him grin in glee at my reaction. He wants me frightened. Needs my terror. Feeding perversely off my helplessness.

"A shame I wasn't allowed to touch your face," he murmurs. Gripping my jaw, he forces my chin around when I try to look away. A finger pushes into the corner of my mouth the taste of him hits my tongue and makes me gag. "My Master wants to see you personally, and he so does hate it when my plaything's eyes are swollen shut."

Anger sparks. I'm not a toy. This psychopath thinks he can do what he wants with me. Snapping my teeth together, I bite down hard on the digit. My captor hisses with the pain.

"You little bitch." A fist ploughs into my cheek so hard I think I might pass out.

Fingers suddenly snatch my hair so tightly it brings fresh tears to eyes.

"You think you can fight me? You aren't the first," he growls closely to my ear. "Some of my sluts even began to enjoy what I did to them, eventually, but they all ended up the same way."

Dead. He's going to murder me just like he did Susan. Dump my mutilated, naked body somewhere for the authorities to find. Bile rises in my throat as images play in my head.

Screwing my eyes shut, I blot out the sight of him. I should have trusted Mars. He doesn't know where I am. I don't even know where I am. There will be no rescue. Just pain and suffering at my captor's hands until he's done playing with me.

Tweaking my nipple with a cruel hand, he doesn't stop twisting until I yelp.

"Enjoy the next few hours alone in the dark. When I come for you again, the fun really starts."

The weight of him on the mattress lifts.

Shaking, limbs ridged, I listen to the sound of him moving across the room. Only when I hear the clank of a metal door slamming shut do I finally open my eyes. With that comes more hopeless tears.

MARS
Chapter eleven

"Mars?" I'm sure I can hear my name being called somewhere. It's too difficult to distinguish, though, amongst the fog of voices destroying each other within my head. Man, against man, woman against woman, child against child, they're fighting. The accents are no longer strange in nature, but Italian, close to home. A simple thing, such as making a pizza, has descended into a fist fight on the streets close to the Pantheon. The use of the wrong cheese leading to the violent assault of the perpetrator. I'm hearing it all. The rage is vibrating from my very soul and infecting the streets of the city that I love. Gunshots echo, Polizia sirens fill the night's air, and the blue lights of their cars have turned the streets below me into a mirage of flashes. I drop my forehead to the window of my office. It's cold. In a city known for its heat, the windows are freezing just like my heart.

"Mars." The voice comes again, this time with more authority.

"What are we going to do dad?" another voice asks. "It's chaos out there."

"Find her," I whisper to no one in particular.

I'm suddenly pulled backward from the window. With instinct, I call for my spear and prepare to attack, but on spinning around, I'm faced with my father and brothers, Hercules and Apollo. The look of concern on their faces forces me to halt my attack and my weapon to disappear.

"You've found her?"

Apollo shakes his head.

"They aren't at the same place they took the other girl. We have so many people out there searching, but things are a little difficult."

I cock my head. "Difficult?"

My father steps forward and clears his throat.

"Rome is descending into chaos."

I turn my head toward the window as a police helicopter flies loudly past with it's beam focusing down into the tunnels of streets.

"Why?" I ask in a state of confusion. The noises in my head are there, but I don't think I'm fully registering them. I feel numb. How did I even get to my office? I was in my home.

"You don't remember?"

"Remember what?"

My father looks down at my hands, and I follow his gaze. They're bloodied, and bruising is starting to appear.

"You went a little mad and smashed up your apartment. We heard the commotion as we were leaving and came straight back. All you told us was that Vicky was gone, and then, you lost it."

I shut my eyes and try to calm my mind, so I can think

back. I recollect none of this. I don't even feel any pain in my hands, and they look really sore.

"Pluto and Orcus." It suddenly all hits me, and the sense of calm I've had over me for the last few minutes evaporates. "I have to find them." I push my brothers aside, with overwhelming force, and stomp powerfully toward the door. I don't get far, though, because my father calls for his scepter and bangs it down on the ground. In an instant, I'm trapped within a cage of lightning.

"Let me go." I turn around and growl out a warning. My own spear comes to hand and tests the crackling force field around me.

"You know the rules, Mars. We stay away from them."

I bash the cage with my spear.

"They'll know where Vicky is."

"And you think they'll just tell us. You've lost your mind. You want to find the girl, then we need you to calm down and regain control of what is going on in Rome. We're spending all our time sorting the fights and not looking for her. Sort your mind out now." My father is stern in his warning. He's always been controlling over us.

"I won't let them hurt her."

"If you actually get your mind straight for five minutes, you'll see that she's already fighting pain. Beauty is suffering; it's evident all around us."

"Then, let me the fuck out of here, so I can go torture Pluto and Orcus."

"You're not listening to me." My father sighs with irrefutable frustration, and the building echoes his sentiments with a shudder of its own. None of my family move or worry. We've felt enough earthquakes in the past. Each time, they've been a result of my father's moods. During a particularly bad argument with my mother in the year nineteen hundred and eight, seventy-two thousand died when he lost my sister, Diana, to Pluto before she could discover her powers. We've been searching for her ever since, and the woe of the catastrophe he caused weighs heavily on my father. At this very moment, however, he could bring the entire city to its knees, and I wouldn't care. All I'm focused on is getting to Pluto and driving my spear through his rotten head.

"I'll listen to you when you take away your trap, Father. I'm not a caged animal."

"Then stop acting like one," he retorts, and I snarl at him with utter contempt.

"I won't rest until I find Vicky." I bring my spear up and thrust it hard through one of the lightning bolts that binds me. This could break my powerful weapon into pieces, but I'm counting on the fact that it's just as powerful as my father's. He always taught us to be equals. The air crackles and hisses with static energy. My brothers step back, but my father maintains his place.

"Mars, if you do this, you'll be responsible for destroying a world that you admire and adore. Listen to the voices in your head. Don't push them aside for your own selfish needs."

"Selfish needs," I interrupt. "She's a goddess, and he'll be torturing her. It's my job to save her, and Pluto is the only one who knows where she is." I'm growing frustrated with the amount of time it's taking for the bars to sever. I shut my eyes and ears to the arguments my family are giving and concentrate on the hate that's coming from the streets of Rome. Another fight starts; this time over a dropped ticket. A woman assumes it's hers, the man, his. She's calling him names, "Bastard, cunt." He responds in kind, "Whore, bitch."

My head swims. The hatred between them is swelling my power. It's taking over my body with its glory. The call of children bullying another is the final strength that I need, and the bars shatter. In an instant, I'm free and dematerialize from my office before I can be trapped again. Without thought to my destination, I reappear in front of Pluto's desk. The man himself is sitting there. He looks up at me from under thick rimmed glasses. The light above ground has always hurt his eyes so he wears them to dull it. He's roughly the same age as my father, and his looks and build are similar. It's not hard to tell that they were once brothers in blood. The founders of the gods.

"I thought you were brought up with manners, teaching you to knock before you entered the room," he snaps and puts the pen, which he was holding, down onto his desk. Shadowy figures appear around him in protection. I know they're the lost souls of the underworld.

"Don't think they'll protect you from me." I point my spear at him, the tip sitting just under his chin and pressing into the column of his bearded neck. "The only thing I'd ever interrupt would be you raping Persephone."

He laughs.

"She agrees to everything that I do with her. So, if you've come to moan about it again, I suggest you leave before I have security throw you out." He turns his head nonchalantly toward the window. "I hear the city of Rome isn't the best place to be to tonight. Too many at war. You wouldn't know anything about that, would you?"

I take my spear and point it directly at his throat. The shadows around me close in, ready to protect their master.

"You took something of mine. I want it back." My voice is eerily calm. It doesn't show any of the rage going on in my head. The voices are getting louder and louder, the screams increasingly spine-chilling.

"I wasn't aware of that. My apologies if I have." He smirks, and I want to wipe it off his face. "I can assure you, though, that anything here is of my possession."

I press the spear closer to his neck. The shadows start to tangle themselves around my arms, their power strong, but I'm able to resist it for now.

"Give her back."

"Her?" Pluto's eyebrow raises in question. "I took a her?"

"You know what you did. I don't care about the decree that says we can't kill each other's factions for the sake of the Earth. If you don't give her back, I'll hunt every member of your team down and slaughter them. I'm the God of War; you want one, you'll get it."

"Well somebody has got their panties in a twist over this 'her', haven't they? I find that very interesting." Pluto waves his hand and my spear is spun away from his throat and into the wall. I call it back, but his magic keeps it in place. "I think this 'her' you want is someone I definitely need to keep within my protection, if I do indeed have her." Pluto waves his hand again, and my body flies through the air and smacks against the glass of the window. "It's so pretty out there. Look at the police lights; look at the fires that have started, the fights, the anger, the agony. It's like being home. You've created that…all for this woman I'm supposedly holding. It's beautiful." He stalks up to me, and I try to move to attack him, but I'm frozen under his strength. The shadows stalk with him, revealing him to be the personification of the devil that he his. "But then, beauty's what all this is about, isn't it?" He leans forward and whispers close to my ear. "I know who she is. Venus, love and beauty. Too powerful to let you and your father have. It's better that she's destroyed, and I'll be the one to do it. Your feelings for her are a bonus. They allow me to bring the underworld to the surface. Don't fight the anger that you're feeling Mars; let it consume you, take over you mind. I wonder how bad it will be when I finally kill her." He laughs, and the air reverberates with his demonic darkness. I want to fight back against him, but my strength is waning. "Look at the trees, Mars, and the grass. It's dying. The beauty of this land, which you love, is being destroyed. She's coming into her powers. Her emotions from the pain she's suffering is destroying the world. If you think I'll give her back to you, then you're surely mistaken. I'll keep her alive and take a piece of her, for as long as I can, until hell on Earth appears."

I let out a massive cry of anguish and frustration. I want to snap Pluto's neck. He may be my uncle, but I want him dead. Rid the Earth of his malevolence and leave it in peace.

Pluto addresses his shadows next.

"Take him back to his father. He's not ready for me, yet."

I go to argue with Pluto, as I find his words really strange, but I'm thrust through space to my father's office. The shadows drop me in front of him, and my spear lands next to me.

"Pluto sends your trash back to you," they echo before vanishing.

My father looms over me with a stern expression on his face. "Are you going to listen to me, now, so that we can rescue Venus, or not?"

I jump to my feet and prepare to warp back to Pluto. This time, I won't come back empty handed. I'm stopped, though, when a piercing scream cripples me. It's Vicky; I know it is. My father and brother's surround me when I drop back to the floor. Every moment I allow the war to take over my mind, I'm failing her. I collapse down on the floor, my eyes shut as I try to listen for her again.

"Mars?" My father touches my shoulder, and I look up at him.

"Help me find her, please."

"Calm you mind," my father urges. "Stop the fighting in Rome before it's destroyed beyond recognition."

I settle my mind, and for the first time since I found Vicky missing, there's silence in my head, peace, except for the soft whimpers of the woman I need to rescue and protect.

VENUS
Chapter twelve

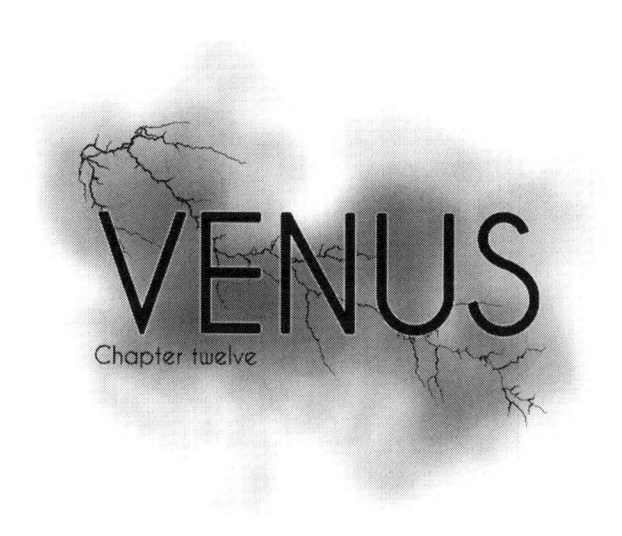

I can't block out the screams. Her eyes screwed shut, and with sobs mirroring my own. Susan. Naked and bound, writhing in pain as the monster thrusts into her again and again.

Every single second of her suffering is there running in a loop on the electronic tablet screen.

My captors' sick fun is to make me endure it. When I could bear to watch it no longer and looked away, he just laughed and raised the volume.

I have no clue how many hours I've had to suffer this. Alone. Terrified. Body pulsing with bruises and the wounds inflicted from the smack of his belt. The blood stopped oozing. I know if left untreated, I could get an infection. Maybe that's how he wants me to go. Slowly and in agony.

Bolts scrape against metal.

Raising my eyelashes, I look toward the door.

Instead of my captor, a man in an elegant suit stalks into the room with a confident ease. Handsome, tanned, his dark hair is sprinkled in places with grey. Brown eyes meet mine. There's something about them, a coldness that sends a chill through my veins. He doesn't look surprised to see me.

Any thoughts of help die.

"Vicky." A smile curves his lips beneath his trimmed mustache. "It's a pleasure to meet you, at last. My name is Pluto, God of the Underworld."

"Please, just let me go."

Thrusting his hands in the pockets of his trousers, he surveys me at leisure. "You're far too valuable for that, my dear. No. We can't have you running back to Mars. Not now when things have started to get interesting."

Swallowing, I try to draw moisture into my parched throat. "What things? What are you talking about?"

"Snatching you is driving him over the edge. The God of War is on a rampage. Rome is in chaos. Blood is being spilt on the streets. The human population is in turmoil. It's glorious."

Mars has done all that?

Shifting in my chains, I wince as pain shoots through my sides.

"Soon, it'll consume him," Pluto continues, glee in his tone. "He'll turn to his darker nature, and then he'll be mine."

I shake my head weakly. "No. He won't do that. Not for me."

"Oh, but he will." Leaning down, he runs his fingers up my bare leg to my curl covered mound. "The Goddess of Love and Beauty holds him and his feelings in the palm of her hand."

The touch makes me flinch. "You're just as warped as the other guy. I don't have any power over anyone."

Pluto chuckles. "Ah yes, Mario. My pet psychopath

enjoyed playing with your friend so much." His dark eyes flick up to the tablet positioned on a table beside the bed. The scenes of my friend's rape and torture unfolding over and over. "He can't wait to get started on you properly."

His words send my stomach into knots. As fear clutches my heart, my breathing becomes fast and swallow. "No."

"Oh yes. But unlike Susan, he's allowed to drag this out. I want you to truly suffer and Mars to feel every delicious second. When your mind and body are finally broken, only then will you be allowed death." Cupping my breast his fingernails bite into the supple flesh. "Sex with you, Venus, is rumored to be life changing. Maybe I'll give your cunt a try before I slit your throat, just so see what all the fuss is about."

I can't escape. Curling inside myself, I try to hide from his malicious laughter. They're going to destroy me. All on a certainty that I have some kind of control over the God of War.

Whimpers leave my cracked lips, but I focus on Mars' face. The power of his aura. How he held me safely.

Footsteps register. Glancing toward the door, I find my torturer has returned.

"Master." Lowering his head, he gives Pluto a respectful loving look.

The God of the Underworld smiles. "No rushing, Mario. I want you to have fun but no killing her. That pleasure will be mine, but anything else your sick little mind comes up with goes."

"Thank you, oh great one."

Turning back in my direction, Pluto's eyes burn through me. "I'll see you again soon, Venus." With that, he vanishes.

Mario looms over the stinking, dirty mattress. Bare

chested streaks of red are dried across his flesh. Blood? The smell is metallic.

He grins when he sees I've noticed them. "From another slut down here. She didn't like it so much when I played with my knife."

Bile rises in my dry throat. I want to scream but I know it's useless. There's no one to help me. I'm in Hell, and there's no way out.

Moving to the electronic tablet, he switches off the video. "Time to make our own film. You're going to be the star, and when we're done, we'll send it to Mars."

"You're sick," I croak.

Ignoring me, he jabs buttons until my image is clear on the screen.

Skin pale, the abuse on my naked body is clear for anyone who watches it to see.

Hands moving to the buttons on his jeans Mario eagerly strips down. Cock bobbing up the tip glistens with precum.

This isn't happening….I keep chanting in my head. Panic building, I twist in my bonds only adding to the bruises they've already caused.

"Don't look so frightened," he tells me, grabbing a fistful of my tangled hair. "You'll like this bit."

Positioning my straining neck, he pushes the tip against my lips. "Open up. If you do a good job, I won't cut off your tits."

I don't want to obey, but I also don't want to feel his blade ripping through my skin. On a whimper, I comply.

Hard, salty, his manhood is shoved roughly into my mouth.

I gag when it hits the back my throat. Without warning, he begins to thrust vigorously.

"Oh yeah. That's it," he growls. "Keep your eyes open let the audience see how much you're enjoying giving me head." Yanking my locks, he makes sure everything is being recorded.

I stare into the camera with a tormented gaze. I don't want this, but what choice do I have? What will Mars think when he sees it? Will he truly slip into something evil? I don't want to be the cause of so much death and misery.

A tear trickles from the corner of my eyes as Mario fucks my mouth.

He doesn't last long. With several sharp pumps, he groans, letting his cum stream onto my tongue. Pulling out, he makes it dribble from my lips to collect on my chest.

Coughing, spluttering, I heave in air.

Giving a sigh of contentment, he gathers a wad of tissue paper from the table to wipe himself clean.

Retching, I spit his semen, trying desperately to rid myself of his vile taste.

"Not bad," he tells me. "Better than your friend Susan. She was all teeth. Of course, she stopped using them after I sliced off a couple of fingers." Swiveling to the camera, he runs his thumb over his bottom lip. "Did you like the show Mars? Want to see some more? Want to hear her plead?"

Snatching something off the table, he stalks around the mattress to my legs.

"No, please, no."

Mario's knife glints in the flaming torch light, a flash of deadly silver.

Crawling onto the end of the bed, he moves between my thighs.

With the restraints so tight, I can't close them to protect myself, and from his smirk, he knows it too.

"This pussy belongs to us now." He directs his words toward the tablet that's still recording. "And it should be marked as such."

Back bowing, a scream breaks from my lips as pain slices through my groin. I feel every second as he cuts through my sensitive flesh.

Hand pressed on my stomach, he holds me down mercilessly.

It feels like eternity before he finishes, and even then, the agony remains, my skin wet with the fresh blood.

Ignoring my crying and whimpering, he eagerly clambers away from me and back to his electronic toy. Grabbing it, he moves back to hold it over where he worked.

Pluto. The name is carved in oozing red just above my blonde curls. A brand of ownership.

"The next time we make a video, she's going to have my cock in her pussy and, then, her ass." Mario boasts, voice shaking with sexual excitement. "I hope you'll be looking forward to it, Mars. I wouldn't want you to miss it." Bringing the device up to my face, he holds it above me. "Anything to say to your boyfriend, Vicky?"

"Please." I can't hide my hopelessness. "Don't let them win, Mars. It doesn't matter about me." The words come out broken. "Don't let Rome fall with death and destruction. You're stronger than that."

My captor gives a snort. Jabbing the button, he ends the recording. "So pathetic. Hell on earth is destined, and your pretty little speech won't change a thing."

Twisting my face away from him, I stare at the wall.

MARS
Chapter thirteen

Vicky's screams send shivers all down my spine. The fear and horror in her eyes has my mind calling for destruction. I want to rain down retribution on the society that gave birth to a man who can do those vile things to another person. Humanity is dead. My father shuts his laptop down, and the video stops playing. I welcome the peace to my ears, but the vision of her suffering is forever imprinted on my retinas. It'll haunt me, even though I can't see it anymore.

"Did anyone recognize anything about the surroundings?" My father asks and looks first at me, but when I just raise an incredulous eyebrow at him to say did he actually expect me to see anything apart from Vicky being forced to swallow another man's dick, he diverts his attention to my brothers. "Apollo, Hercules?"

Apollo speaks first, "It's a church. It seems familiar. I need to think."

"Take your time. We've got all day." My voice drips with sarcasm. "I'm sure being a human he can't get it up again for at least another hour. It's not like he could be raping her as we speak."

"Mars." The tone in which my father says my name tells me to control my anger. He's fighting a lost cause, though.

"It's a church. We only have in excess of nine hundred of them here in Rome. What are we waiting for?" I reply and slam my fist on the desk. The silence that has existed in my head for a short time now erupts with the growls of a fight. It's a joyous sound. At least someone is doing something and not debating their fate."

"I thought you'd pulled your head out of your ass. I see it's gone back in." My father pushes my hands off his desk and steps in front of me. I get to my feet, and we stand nose to nose. "Hercules, take him up to the heavens. His stupidity is causing us to risk losing Venus."

"I'm not going anywhere," I snap and shake my brother off when he grabs my arm. Hercules may be known for his strength, but we're actually equals on that score.

"Then think," my father spits at me. "We know that church, feel her, sense her, recognize the features around her and not the suffering she's experiencing. She's close to death....I feel it. I know every time a human god dies. Ironically, that's the only time they're revealed to me. Unless we stop this now, you will lose her."

I don't know why I'm struggling so much with my emotions. I've always been so strong and controlled before. It seems as though being inside Vicky has given me an empathy I've never had before. I've known right and wrong all my life, yes, but I've swayed toward the latter in a bid to rid the world of war. Of all the god's, I'm the ticking time bomb. By losing my mind, I destroy the Earth. I have to focus. I motion for my father to lift the laptop lid again. He does so and restarts the video. This time, I focus on Vicky's surroundings with all my strength and concentration. I know that if I look at her face, then I'll lose myself again. I can't do that. The voices of violence quieten in my head, and all I hear are Vicky's sobs.

"Don't let Rome fall; don't let them win. I see the truth of what this city is, now. Its beauty's in the lines of history that are everywhere. Fight for it, Mars, please."

My breath hitches, there's no noise coming from the computer-tablet. No, it's in my head instead. My eyes widen, and I stare at my father.

"She's finding her power," he exclaims. "You hear her?"

I nod dumbfounded and look at the screen. Skulls are everywhere on the paused image. I examine their eerie presentation. The sound of an explosion echoes through my thoughts, and we all look toward the window. A building has exploded–flames erupt in the night sky. I blink a few times. A battle cry sounds in my head, and I wince at the loudness of it.

"Mars, you have to stay with us," my father implores. He's finished being angry at me. He's desperate, now. His worry for his family, the humans, and Rome twisting in his gut. I look back to the computer screen, and my brain scans through all the places in Rome. I see the city as if flying above it, darting in and out of places with a skillful weave. As I approach the Barberini, my body begins to weigh heavier. I can feel myself sinking into the floor. The buildings are crumbling, the edges jagged like a half-eaten biscuit. The water in the fountain square is green and moldy. This isn't normal. The beauty of this place is breaking down. That's it, the key to finding Vicky She's the Goddess of Beauty and Love. Her powers are coming to her. If I follow the souring of the land to its source, I'll find her. My heart rate picks up, and I hear, softly in the background of my mind, the encouragement of my father and brothers. I fly a little higher in my mind, and I see the *Santa Maria della Concezione dei Cappuccini*. The skulls! That's it. The crypt to the church is littered with them. My mind comes back to my body, and I blink a few times.

"She's at *Santa Maria della Concezione dei Cappuccini*." I tell my family, holding my hand out for my spear and dematerialize before my father can stop me.

In no time at all, I'm at the church and bursting through the door. It's late, so even though the city is always busy, it's quiet in this place as most worshippers are asleep. That's why he chose it. My father and brothers appear at my side ready for the battle. My father holds his lightening bolt, Hercules his daggers, and Apollo his harp. I've always wondered about his choice of weapon. I guess I'm about to find out. A scream comes from below us, and I gasp out loud when blood starts to run down the walls of the church.

"We don't have much time. Stay together," my father orders. "We don't know which, if any, of Pluto's men are down there."

I take one look at him, ignore him, and charge for the crypt. My only thought is to stop the pain that Vicky's in. She should not get her powers this way. It should be enlightening within the trials that she receives them. Not as a result of torture. My family keeps pace with me, and we all descend the stairs toward the crypt. A shallow river of blood has filled the floor. I start to worry that it isn't the mirage of a goddess coming into her power but from Vicky's actual body. There's so much of it. A blood-curdling scream has us kicking open the door. The man who I failed to have sent to prison for life is standing in front of Vicky with his foul dick in his hands. His head turns to the side as we enter, and he goes as white as a sheet.

"You wanted a war you got one," I snarl and step into the room.

"Pluto! Orcus!" The man calls out.

"I think you'll find you've been abandoned."

In an instant, I project myself directly in front of him and thrust my spear through his chest. A thousand voices call out in triumph throughout Rome. I twist and turn the magical weapon, wringing every last ounce of shock and pain out of the vile man before pulling the spear out. He falls to the floor in death. I take my spear and stab it directly into his groin, severing his shriveled-up dick in the process.

"Enough," my father orders. "See to Vicky."

Voices rage in my head; I can't stop them. They're calling for more blood: for Pluto's and Orcus' heads. I silence them, for now. Vicky's soft whimpers capture my attention, and I turn to her. She's tied steadfast to the altar. With a wave of my hand, the binds are cut, and she's free.

"Mars," she whispers. Her body is battered and broken. I can smell the man I've just killed, his vile scent, all over her. I bring her into my arms and to my chest. She hesitates at first but then relaxes at my familiarity.

"You're safe," I whisper and ignore the fact that her touch on my skin no longer ignites passion but a lust for retribution and the blood of the underworld.

VENUS
Chapter fourteen

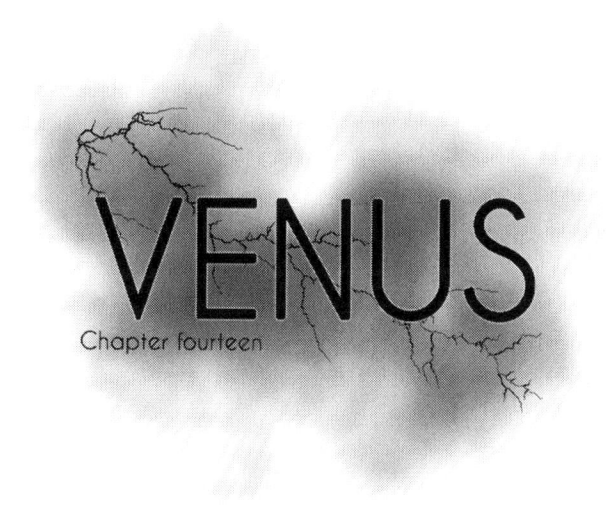

The voices ebb in and out. I'm so cold it feels like ice is living in my veins. I can barely feel my body.

"We're too late."

"No."

"Mars, calm yourself. Your brother's wrong, but she hovers between life and death."

The arms around me tighten. A haven of heat I know, now, that holds no fear. Not anymore.

"What must I do?" His voice is low and urgent.

Forcing my eyelids open, I focus on his handsome face. A darkness lurks just beneath the surface. Lips pressed in a thin white line, an urgent tick is beating in his jaw.

"Take her to the sea. Let the ocean soothe her," another familiar voice speaks.

"She's in no fit state…"

"We're losing her," the other older male cuts him off. "You must show her the beauty of the world again. Show her the love."

Beauty? There's nothing beautiful left here. Nothing but emptiness, pain, and a hopelessness that I can sense causing me to slip away. Susan is gone. In my heart, I know I'm going to join her. After what Mario did, I'm not sure I want to continue on. Not with Pluto waiting in the wings ready to snatch me at every turn.

"Vicky, hold on." Mars' words are soft. Lips brush my cheek, stealing a sigh from my own.

The chill in the air recedes.

Through the blackness, which is intent on claiming me, it takes a second for the sound of waves to register. Warm and sultry, the Mediterranean breeze drifts against my battered flesh. I lie limp in his arms as he gently carries me. Did he use his powers? Wherever we are, I know it's better than the cell. At least I won't die somewhere echoing with my misery and pain. Flopping against him, nothing registers but the male talking to me so softly. What he's saying is noise. My brain unable to string it together to make any sense.

A hiss escapes me when wetness laps around my ankles. As I startle, I find myself immersed. Throbbing, the open wounds over every inch of my naked body begin to scream as salt water burns.

"Easy, Vicky, easy," Mars croons, his nose nuzzling my cheek. "Let it heal you."

Air stutters in my lungs. It's too much. Everything. Crushing me from the inside, it builds. I can't do this. I'm not strong enough. Not enough. I couldn't save my friend. Couldn't save myself. How can I be a goddess? I'm weak.

A mouth claims mine: hard, insistent.

My panic and pain both morph into bliss.

Mars kisses me as if I'm the only thing that exists. Hot,

passionate. Arms wrapped around me, he keeps me pressed to the hard planes of his muscles, beneath his suit.

Hands sliding up to the nape of his neck, I devour him just as keenly.

Tongues dance and entwine. Our bodies strain together as the waves crash against the beach beneath a sky filled with stars.

"Bella, don't leave me." It's a groan as he scatters quick kisses over my upturned face.

Clawing at the edges of his soaked shirt, I rip the sides apart. Perfect, toned abs meet my searching fingers.

I want him. Need him. If I don't have him now, I'll die.

Hands fumbling with his belt, his own slide over mine.

"Please." The word is a whine. A plea.

Brown, intense eyes meet my imploring gaze. I let him see how much I desire this. Somehow, we managed to get his clothes off. Unfastening his pants, he shoves them down the length of his legs. Kicking them free with his shoes, he stands before me, gloriously naked. Winding my arms around his chest, I draw him back with me. The water embraces us, cradles our forms as if we were its lovers. Close. Intimate as I hold this dark war god close to my breast. Finding his cock, I curl my fingers around its girth. Pulsing, thick, it jerks in my firm grip. A moan is torn from Mars' lips. Eagerly, I lift up, winding my legs around the leanness of his hips. With one sure push, I spear myself on his hardness. He fills me with one thrust.

Panting, shaking, we remain locked for what feels like a lifetime, but I know only seconds pass. His hands find my ass. Clutching tightly, he begins to move in me. Head tipping back, I ride him with abandonment. It's almost too much, the way the sensations overwhelm me. The lap of the cleansing water as it tingles over my skin, heals the wounds and damage I endured at Mario's hands.

"I thought I'd lost you," Mars confesses close to my ear.

It makes my heart clench. "I thought...I was going to die."

Holding him closely, I tangle my fingers in his hair. I don't want to relive the horror or be dragged backward into the nightmare. All I want is this gift. Mars' possession. The way he sweeps everything that's happened aside and makes me forget. As our rhythm changes, the pace becoming faster, our moans and groans mingle.

"Yes, yes, yes!" My lust filled shout is lost in the sound of the surf. "Mars!"

Then, I feel it, the delicious tightening deep inside. As my pussy walls spasm, I lose myself in a blissful release.

Mars grunts, his own body still pumping into me. There's no gentleness here. It's primal. Wild.

"Vicky!" His tortured cry sends him over.

Gripping my hips mercilessly, he spills his essence deep within my core. I'm mush. The ability to think gone as I lie dazed, floating in the safety of his arms.

MARS

Chapter fifteen

The water of the cerulean blue sea laps at my ankles. They're entwined with Vicky's as she lays with her head against my chest. Neither of us feel the cold of the hazy morning. Her breathing is steady, but I know she doesn't sleep for she murmurs her thoughts occasionally. She's healing physically; emotionally, it'll take longer to recover from all that she's lived through these last few days. My own mind is calmer than it has been in hours. I don't hear wars raging in Rome, just the peace of the early morning and the sun rising in glorious hues of red, orange, yellow, and purple.

"Why did Mario do this?" She shifts and sitting up a little, she looks at me. Her eyes are tired but still so full of questions.

"He was warped in his mind. We can't figure out any other reasons," I reply calmly and take in a long breath of the fresh sea air.

"There was another man who came to see me. He said he was the God of the Underworld, Pluto?"

This time the noise that comes from my mouth is more of a strangulated groan.

"Did he touch you?"

"No. He told me he would come back and kill me. That I was too valuable to release because of what you were doing to Rome." She cocks her head in question.

"You should probably avoid the news today. There maybe one or two hundred tales of skirmishes erupting in Rome. My father will see what he can do to smooth things over."

"So, people don't question that a god made them go crazy?"

"Something like that. As gods, we're tied to our emotions, and they affect the places we are in. It's how I found you."

"I don't understand?" She lays her head back down on my broad chest. The weight of the tiredness in her body too heavy to hold up any longer.

"Did Pluto say anything about what god he thinks you are?"

"He called me Venus? Isn't she the Goddess of Beauty and Love?"

"She is; you are."

She sits bolt upright.

"I thought he was nuts calling me that, but he wasn't was he? You think it as well?"

"Search inside yourself, Vicky. Your powers are already coming to the forefront of your subconscious mind. All around that church you were in was rotting, the water turning rancid. It was you who was doing that, nobody else. Your terror at the situation you were in was destroying the earth around you. I was blinded by hate and revenge for those who took you, and Rome suffered a night where fires, gunshots, and sirens filled the air. It's the same. We're linked to the planet we're on. Pluto knows this and wants to use our abilities to destroy the humans and bring us back out of hiding. That can't ever happen, though. We have to protect their peace, keep ourselves hidden."

Vicky looks down to the sand underneath us. She stretches her hand out and runs her fingers through the glassy granules.

"That's why you brought me here?" She moves her gaze up and around at the stunning scenery in front of us. The cobalt blue of the ocean, the craggy cliffs of the coastline descending into the horizon with sightings of white villas dotted infrequently. "The beauty of it started the healing process. The love that you have for me completed it."

"War and beauty combined can be a powerful vessel."

She lays back down and pulls away from me. Her body seems smaller as she curls up into a ball.

"I can't...I don't even know where to start with all of this. It's so much to take in. I don't know what's real, or what isn't anymore. Who's a god and who isn't. Who's good; who's evil. I'm so tired and so confused. I'm scared to shut my eyes because I might see what he did to me? I want to scrub my body clean to take away his marks from my flesh, my mouth, my mind. And he wasn't even a god. He was a normal man, and you couldn't stop him doing that to my friend or to me." Tears tumble down her cheeks. It takes everything I have within me not to reach out and wipe them away. These are tears that needed to be shed. The emotion of her suffering washing away into the sand.

"The wounds will heal. I know the pain seems too real and familiar, but I'm going to help you."

"I want to go back to England, to the time before I got on the plane. To forget all this happened."

"You know that can't ever happen, now."

"Why not?" she shouted. "None of you knew about me until I came to Italy. I was quietly getting on with my life in Devon. I can go back to that."

I shake my head.

"Even if my father would let you go, I wouldn't."

"You're not in charge of me," she snapped.

"No, I'm not. But our bodies have shared so much together that you'd never be able to sleep at night without feeling me inside you. You'll never be able to love without your heart beating only for me. You'll see something of beauty and wonder if you created it. If you get angry, then the darkness will descend, and that beauty will fade to something foul. It's the way it will be until the day your human body dies. Then, you will be reborn, and the process will start again, memories will reside in your head of a man you love. Of a place so breathtaking that it'll capture your breath, despite the fact that you've never seen it. You can't escape this, now, even if you want to. The process has started. Pluto will chase you to the ends of the Earth to take you into his world and exploit your love and beauty for his own nefarious ends. And you are so far under my skin, I'll haunt your every turn because I won't be able to keep away. Your essence swims in my veins. It drowns me in its virility. I'm under Beauty's spell, and there's no way to break it now."

Vicky unfurled herself from the ball and brought her hand to mine.

"I'm scared."

"I know"–bringing her hand up to my lips, I kiss it tenderly– "You're tired. Let's go back to my house in Tuscany and get some sleep. We can think more on this in the morning."

"I don't know if I'll sleep."

"You will if I'm wrapped around you for protection."

"You won't leave me?"

"I just said. You're under my skin, and it's not possible for me to leave you."

"Ok."

I transport us to my bedroom within the extensive villa that I own in Tuscany. It's nestled in the hills of Val d'Orcia and surrounded by vineyards. It's peace and tranquility personified and so secure. Even a mouse could not run along my land without me knowing about it, for Bellona and my son live in a separate villa on these lands. Pluto will have no chance of finding Vicky here. I just have to hope that Bellona and Vicky have no opportunity to meet each other during our stay.

We materialize in my bedroom, and I help Vicky to remove her clothes and settle in the bed. I sit on the edge.

"Are you not coming to bed?"

"I have a few calls I need to make, first. I'll get the phone and come back and join you soon. I'll leave the door open. Pluto can't get you here. You have my word that it's secure. If you want, I can call for someone to watch you while I do that?"

She shakes her head, her heavy eyelids drooping.

"I'm not leaving you until you're asleep. I promise I'll be just outside the door when you are, so I won't disturb you."

She yawns. Her body's obvious need for sleep overruling the fear she has of trying to do so.

"Be quick," she murmurs, and her eyelids flutter shut.

They don't open again, and her breathing shallows. I kiss the top of her head and make a silent vow of protection.

Going as quickly as I can, I strip out of my still wet clothes and pull on a pair of track pants. I retrieve my house phone from the lounge, all the while listening out for even the slightest noise coming from the bedroom. I dial my father.

"How is she?" he answers after the first ring.

"Sleeping. Her wounds are healing, but she's confused. We're at my villa in Val d'Orcia. I want to keep as much beauty around her as I can. How is Rome?"

"You certainly did a number on it? We can't keep it out of the newspapers. People are asking why war nearly broke out here last night? I think in the light of a fresh day, though, we can spin it as a few criminals caused issues, not the majority. Maybe wipe out a few people that we need to get rid of."

I laugh, knowing that my father means the cases where we're in direct opposition to Pluto.

"He was there. He's knows who she is," I tell my father.

"Pluto?"

"Yes."

"She may have to face the trials sooner rather than later. She needs her powers. He won't stop coming for her, now. Not after he tasted Hell on Earth last night."

"I know," I reply lamentably. "She's not ready, just yet, though. A few more days to recover. The beauty within her is scarred. I fear she'll only be at greater risk of achieving Pluto's wishes by forcing the trials on her."

"Alright. Take a few days with her. Work with her and teach her more about what we are. See if she can gain control of the powers she has developing."

"I will do."

"Mars?"

"Yes."

"How are you?" The question takes my breath away. My father has always cared for us but to know that he's still so worried, after many millions of years, shatters my own exhausted body. I slump back against the wall outside my room.

"Did people die?" I ask.

My father pauses before he answers.

"Yes."

"Innocent."

Another pregnant pause.

"Yes."

I swallow deeply.

"I'm sorry."

"Work through the guilt, now. You can't hold it in because it'll destroy you. Out of all my sons, your power is the most volatile and likely to cause chaos. You've been strong up until now. Keep that within you."

"I will," I reply, wondering how the hell I'm supposed to do that, knowing that I've, yet again, killed those who didn't deserve it.

"Call me later."

"Night."

I hang up.

Sleep is calling me as well, now. I look to where Vicky is peaceful in my bed. She's stunningly angelic in her beauty. It takes my breath away, every time I look at her. I put the phone down on a chest of drawers when I enter the room and climb in the bed next to her. I wrap myself around her, and she turns to nestle her head against my chest. I shut my eyes to sleep, but all I see is the agony of those who died:

faceless figures bleeding and weeping. All because my emotions have led to their end.

This battle with Pluto has gone on long enough. It needs to end, and I'll be the one to finish it. I'm the God of War after all.

VENUS

Chapter sixteen

The nightmare rips me from sleep. Eyes snapping open, I lie shaking, terrorized I'm still back in the cell. Mario's stinking breath against my face as he whispers obscene things.

It takes a few minutes to realize my surroundings. A bedroom, open, airy.

The weight of an arm slung possessively over my stomach also registers.

Mars.

Turning my head, I examine his handsome sleeping face. He looks younger when relaxed, at peace. As if whatever responsibilities he carries on his shoulders during his waking moments have slipped away.

Hair tousled, he's so deeply asleep I wonder if he's experienced the same bone deep weariness that claimed me.

Do I love him? Is he right?

With everything happening so fast, can I trust this feeling I have in my heart? This unstoppable attraction between us? Or is it an illusion? Something to bind us together because of what I'm supposed to be? The Goddess of Love and Beauty. An ancient being. His opposite. What I feel is fierce. It's all consuming when we are together, taking me over.

As gently as I can, I move his arm and wiggle from the bed.

Watching him just to be sure I don't disturb him, I can't help my attention drift down to the sculpted muscles of his bare chest and his tanned, firm skin. The thin sheet barely covers his groin.

He's perfectly posed in slumber, one arm tossed carelessly above his head, the other resting over his stomach. Strong, yet vulnerable.

My fingers twitch in response, desperate to draw him. To lovingly create the picture before me with an artist's eye. With it comes the painful reminder of the last time I'd sketched. The night Susan and I were taken. I'm not sure I'll ever get pleasure from my artwork again. It's just another piece of myself that's been ripped out.

Tearing myself away, I grab the white robe, which has been left idly draped over a wicker chair. The second I thread my arms through it, a masculine scent envelopes me. God, he smells so good. It sends a flutter through my pussy.

Padding from the room, I slowly begin to explore my new surroundings.

Spacious, clean, the villa has the perfect blend of modern and country style. Beyond the windows, rows of lush green vines, heavy with grapes, roll along the landscape. A vineyard. It's breathtaking and remote. The perfect place to hide.

I should have known Mars' house in Tuscany wouldn't be something simple. The whole place screams money.

Finding a glass, I fill it with tap water. I need it to rinse the bitter taste left in my mouth from the dream. It goes someway to easing my parched throat. The thought of food repels me. I know I should eat, but I can't face that right now. I crave something else.

Quietly as I can, I unlock the front door and step out into the sunlight. Its heat hits my skin, sultry and baking. Freedom. Inhaling deeply, I savor the fresh summer air.

After being confined and tortured... I thought I'd never experience something so simple again. As my mind starts to slide toward memories I want to keep buried, I wrap my arms around my waist.

I don't want to remember. Not now. Not ever. My body may be miraculously healed, but the scars that remain in my mind are left festering. They've changed me. I'm no longer the same woman I was. Shadows linger in my thoughts. Darkness.

Barefoot, I move aimlessly toward the nearest row of vines. Beneath my soles, I savor the feel of the hard-packed earth. It's real. Something to focus on.

The earthy scent of the soil soothes my fears.

It's such a peaceful place. Only me, the sounds of nature, and the plants that flourish so lovingly here.

Houses are dotted here and there along the horizon. Black silhouettes. Families who work the land? Mars must employ people to gather his crops. To make the wine. Maybe he has a well-known brand for all I know.

A sound disturbs me. It's small, subtle, but makes my heart race as I spin to face it.

Hand pressed to my chest and dread cramming my thoughts, I'm not prepared for the boy.

Standing a few feet away, he observes me with curiosity in his bright brown eyes. Dark hair curls around his young face. It's his features that capture my attention. The resemblance to Mars is stunning. He has to be at least twelve or thirteen years old.

"Buongiorno," he murmurs, dipping his head in a nod.

Licking my dry lips, I try to recover my voice. Buongiorno."

"Ti sei perso?"

"I don't understand," I reply, fingers lacing together. "I don't speak Italian."

"Are you lost?"

"I...no I'm staying with a... friend."

His brows pinch together as he studies me some more. He's curious about the bathrobe I'm wearing. "This is my father's land. Nobody's supposed to wander around here without permission but me and my Mother. Even someone as pretty as you."

His father? Any hopes that this could be Mars younger brother fades into dust. A son. He has a son. And maybe a wife? Pain knives inside my fragile heart, making me wince.

How could he fuck me when he has a family? When he's married with a child?

The knowledge sends the shards of darkness digging inside me a little deeper.

Mars' words echo in my head. How he can't let me go. His beautiful poetic speech on the beach. More secrets. More lies. Is anyone actually telling me the truth?

"Are you ok?"

The soft concern brings me back to the awareness of the boy. "Yes, I'm sorry. I'm not feeling too well. The heat," I lie.

I avoid his gaze. It's almost too much to bear to look at him.

"You're English with pale skin. You're not used to the Italian sun." Stepping closer, he offers me his hand. "Come,

I'll take you somewhere cooler. A place where you can have a cold drink."

Panic sets in, but I push it aside. There had been no signs of anyone else living at Mars' villa. It can't be the main house.

"I should get back to my...friend," I tell him with a small smile.

His frown deepens, making him so much more like his father that it makes me heart clench. "As you wish."

On stiff legs, I turn and walk away further from the house and the man I've left sleeping.

Even the thought of letting his son see me return there is repulsive. I couldn't do that to the boy. It wouldn't be fair. His father might be a bastard, but the child is innocent. I'd never hurt anyone intentionally. It would be far too cruel.

Trekking past vine after vine, I don't stop until the gaze on my back lessens and finally ebbs. Even then, I keep walking. I don't want to go back. The pain only sharpens. I'm lost in a world I don't recognize anymore. Emotions churn up inside me, and I feel the dampness rolling down my cheeks. I want to be numb. Why do I have to feel so much? Each blow hurts with something new. I need something stable. Normality. Even if it's wrong and leaves me aching, I want to go home. I might love Mars, but I won't be second in his heart. A hidden pleasure to visit when his wife is away. What I need is to distance myself. Lock down everything. Keep it contained until I'm somewhere I can curl up and face each and every jagged agonizing truth. Pluto still hunts me. Leaving now would be suicide. Once everything is resolved, I'll make my escape.

Ignoring the sweat as it pours down my face along with my tears, I follow my feet wherever they lead me.

MARS
Chapter seventeen

I stir in the bed and reach out to bring Vicky into my arms but find only empty space. My heartbeat accelerates as I sit bolt upright and adjust my still sleepy eyes to my surroundings.

"Vicky?" I call with nervousness that an answer won't come, and when it doesn't, I'm out of my bed and into the hallway of my villa.

"Vicky?" I shout louder this time, but still, no answer comes.

"Fuck." My legs take me down the stairs at a rapid pace. The front door is wide open. I'm out of it and shouting her name loud enough to wake the dead.

"Papa." Luigi appears at my side, his brows furrow together when he looks at me, "Why are you naked?"

I drop my head and realize that I've coming running out of the house butt naked. I place my hands over my groin.

"It's one of those weird adult things that we don't talk about piccolo." I shrug my shoulders, and he just narrows his eyes further. For a child of twelve, my son is bright enough to know what is going on in the world. He knows that his mother and father aren't in a relationship and accepts that we will never be. He still has the best of both worlds, though, with us living so close to each other most of the time. He's also adored by his grandparents as he was their first grandchild. He doesn't have specific powers as his mother and I do, for he doesn't rule over anything, but he's learning and will be a strong warrior in the future. "You haven't seen a strange woman wandering around, here have you?" I ask.

"You mean the woman who wasn't wearing a lot and walking around your vineyards? I told her that she shouldn't be in them. I know you don't like it." He screws his face up–it still has a little of his puppy fat around the edges. "She's a funny one. I knew she came from your villa. She said she was sick and going to return to you, but she went off on a funny path. I think she's probably got lost in the vines. Are all woman that strange, papa? I know mama is at times. I'm so glad I'm a boy."

I can feel myself physically relax with every word my son speaks. I even end up with a big smile on my face at the end of the conversation. But then, I realize that she's seen him. I look over to the vineyards and instantly notice the point where she met him. The grapes have soured and shriveled up. I sigh.

"Women are always going to be funny creatures," I tell my son and ruffle the shaggy mop of hair on top of his head. "The fact that you're learning it now will only serve to help you in the future. Run home to your mama, now. I better go and find my strange friend."

"Ok, papa. Can I come over later? I want to show you how much I've been practicing my fighting skills."

"Of course." Luigi turns on his heel and runs off back to the home he shares with his mother on the far side of the vineyard. I may not have love for Bellona, but I'll always be grateful for the son she's given me. It was the best thing that we ever did.

I look down at my naked form and curse the fact I've forgotten clothes. The workers here don't need to see in my birthday suit, but I don't have time to worry too much about it for Vicky appears from in between the vines. She gasps.

"Mars."

I raise an eyebrow at her.

"I'm not sure what to punish you for first, leaving me alone in bed and making me run outside naked, giving everyone a shock at the size of my manhood, or the fact that you've ruined this year's grape stock."

"What?" She turns and looks back at the path she's just walked. "Did I do that?" Her eyes go wide. I can see the traces of tears around the red rims. They look sore from the emotion that had coursed through her in the last few days.

I drop my hands from my groin and stride purposefully to stand before her.

"I think I'll start with the grapes. Yes, the boy you saw is my son. Yes, he lives here with his mother. No, his mother and I aren't together, now. She's a consort of mine. I've been on this planet for a long time, Vicky. I have needs. Gods are highly sexual people. Bellona is one of them. I visited her when I needed an itch scratching. We had a happy accident one day, and Luigi was conceived. It's a common mishap with us. Have I told you that I have roughly nineteen brothers and sisters that I know of, not all with the same mother but all with the same father. When you've been on this Earth as long as we have, accidents will happen." I take a deep breath in the middle of my explanation, and I see Vicky start to sway as she takes everything in. "And this is probably the last thing that you want to hear, but if it stops you from ruining my grapes and the livelihood of the people who live on this land, then I'm not going to keep anything from you. There"–I fold my arms across my chest and Vicky's eyes look down to my cock where it starts to stand to attention just from being near her– "I've said my piece. Do your worst now?"

She brings her top lip into her mouth and sucks on it slightly before letting out a small laugh.

"I've been cursing you my entire walk. Thinking you were married and using me as a bit on the side. I'm sorry about your grapes." She looks down at the ground and twists her foot in the dust slightly. "If I knew how to fix them, I would. I didn't mean to do it."

"I know." I drop my arms to my side and step closer to her. I don't dare bring her into my arms, yet. I need to know she accepts I have a son.

"What did you think of Luigi?" I ask.

"Your son?"

"Yes. His full name is Enyalius, but I call him Luigi. It's easier and makes more sense in this modern world."

"Yes, Enyalius is a bit of a mouthful." She comes closer to me and presses a slender hand onto my chest. My dick bobs higher, hoping for the touch instead. "He looks so much like you. He seems to have the charm with the women as well."

"He's his father's son." I wink. "I'm sorry I didn't tell you about him sooner and that you had to find out this way. I would have told you, eventually. I just wanted to give you some time to adjust to everything else, first."

"It's a lot to take in. All of it." She turns and looks at the vineyards. "Will this sort of thing happen every time?"

"No, you'll get control."

She nods.

A noise to our left has our heads spinning around. One of the maids from my house emerges with a basket of washing in her hands. She sees us and specifically me naked with a hard on and turns bright red.

"Sorry, sir," she blusters and disappears back into the house.

"Will you allow me to take you back into the house before we cause anymore commotion?" I ask, desperately hoping she says yes.

"Please." She drops her head down onto my chest, and before she can object, I've scooped her up into my arms and am striding purposefully back to my bedroom. I sit her on the bed and step back, searching her face for any hint of lies or fear.

"Are you sure you're ok with Luigi?" I ask.

"Yes," she utters. "It's another thing about this new life of mine that I have to adjust too. I won't lie Mars. I'm terrified of what everything means, and at this moment, I'm torn between staying here and running back to England and curling up in a little ball, hoping that everything will just go away. I'm not stupid, though. I know that can never happen, now."

"You'll see England again." I lean forward, stroke her face, and bring my hand to rest at her chin. "How about I take you there this afternoon? You can show me where you live. We can get some of your stuff and bring it here? What do you say?"

"Will your father allow that? Won't it be dangerous?"

"We can take some of my brothers with us," I offer.

"I'd like that."

Her face drops.

"Susan. What happens to her? I have to tell her parents. We have to bury her."

I swallow and shut my eyes.

"I'll help you do all that. My father has her body. Let yourself grieve and adjust first, though. We don't have to rush into anything."

She nods, and her small hand comes out again and touches the tip of my cock. I groan long and loudly at the pleasure surging through my body from her delicate touch.

"I didn't sleep that well last night with nightmares. Mario, and what he did to me echoed through all of them. I need a new memory Mars. What he did to my mouth, I need to forget it."

"No," I whisper. "I don't want you to do anything you don't feel you are ready for."

"I need it," she pleads and grips my cock harder. "Make me forget him. Only you can do that. Only we, together, can repair the memories of the hatred I feel when it comes to him. Bring me beauty; bring me love. Show me how amazing having you in my mouth can be."

She opens her legs, and I settle in between them, so my dick is in her face. We both go silent–no words are needed, now, as I rescue her again.

Her tongue darts out of her mouth and licks at my length. It jumps with delight, and I can already feel my balls tightening. I groan when she wraps her lips around the tip and moves me into her mouth. I curl my fist around her hair and twist, so I can help control her movement. I like my dick sucked roughly, but in this moment, I just need to be in the warmth of her mouth. I don't need her choking on my length. I don't need to see her eyes watering as I cut off her breathing by shoving myself so far down her throat. I'm getting lost in the feeling of her tongue, twirling around the sensitive flesh on my shaft. Her small flicks send fizzles of electricity darting through my body. All of my blood is rushing to my dick, and my head is spinning. I've never experienced this before.

I look down, and my balls tighten when she looks back up at me. Vicky, with my cock in her mouth, is the most beautiful thing in the world.

"You wanted beautiful. You should see how you look to me. I've never seen anything like it before." My own mind is awash with the memories of Mario forcing her to suck him off, but each time she slides up and down my length, they dissipate into nothing. I shift both of us on the bed, so she can see our reflection in a mirror in the corner of my room. I push my hips forward, and my cock slides deeper into her mouth. Her eyes widen as she watches: the lust in them evident.

"Quicker," she mumbles around me, and the vibrations have me gripping her hair tighter and sliding into her quicker. We're both looking in the mirror. I follow every expression on her face as I pump faster and faster. I can feel my orgasm as it winds through my body.

"Vicky, I have to pull out."

"No," she orders, and I push into her one final time and erupt. While my dick is still pulsating, I withdraw and allow my cum to decorate her lips. I lose my breath, stagger back to a chair, and collapse down into it. Her tongue comes out and wipes my essence from her lips. Fuck, I think I'm going to come again, already, just from that one action.

She looks away from the mirror to me. I notice the tears streaming down her cheeks. I'm on my knees for this woman and crawling toward her as quickly as I can. I wrap my arms around her and hold her as tightly as possible.

"Beautiful," she mumbles into my chest. I pull back.

"My Goddess of Beauty," I reply and kiss her. I can taste remnants of myself of her lips. I search her face for any signs of distress, but I find only peace.

"I'm ready, Mars. I want to learn to be the goddess I am."

VENUS

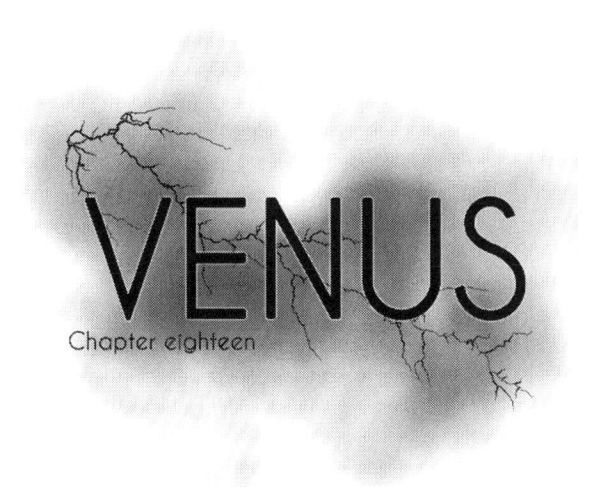

Chapter eighteen

Glancing across the piazza, I observe the people bustling around in the heat of the afternoon sun. Although small, the village is a busy place. A rustic gem tucked away in the Tuscan countryside. It has a certain charm to its laid-back air. The buildings white-walled but welcoming.

With a natural hot spring located a mile outside, it's the perfect spot for tourists and Italians on summer vacation.

Attention returning to the male sitting across from me, I offer him a smile.

He's dressed handsomely in a loose, white cotton shirt and a pair of jeans. Even though he's clothed to blend in, his looks stir attention around us. Men admire him, and women swoon at the perfect specimen of masculinity.

Mars' eyes soften as they meet mine.

"Thank you for bringing me out to lunch," I tell him, lifting the glass of peach iced tea. "This is such a pretty place." Taking a sip, the liquid refreshes me.

"Somewhere you'd like to sketch?" he enquires, mirroring my smile.

I feel my moment of happiness dim. "I'm not sure I'll want to ever draw again. Too many memories."

"Vicky, don't let Mario and Pluto steal this from you. I've seen your work and you're very talented."

Remembering the sketches, I'd drawn of Mars, himself, heat warms my cheeks. I have no idea where they ended up. For all I know, my things and Susan's are still at the hotel: clothes, money, passport. The pretty pale blue summer dress and matching sandals I'm wearing, along with the sexy lacy lingerie, are some things he acquired for me. I have no idea where they came from.

A large hand engulfs mine across the table, bringing me back from my thoughts.

"I'll arrange for new pencils, paint, paper, and anything else you need to be brought here. The best that money can buy. You can turn one of the spare bedrooms into a studio."

He's been nothing but sweet since he found me this morning. I still can't believe he was walking around butt naked.

Mars has a son. I'm still a little uncomfortable at the thought of him having consorts. God knows I never thought he was celibate being an ancient God, but I don't like thinking about the other women he's had sex with. Are they all immortals? How many does he have who he visits? I guess, now, I'm one of them. Is he going to continue seeing them?

"I want to see you smile. When you're unhappy..." His hand squeezes mine.

Following his gaze, I spy the blooms that have withered

into black twisted clumps in a flower box to my left. Knowing I've done that sends a dullness through my heart. I killed them. Destroyed their beauty.

"Maybe we should go." When I try to rise, he tugs me back down.

"No, Vicky. Don't run away. You want to learn to be a goddess, and we can start here."

"I don't want to hurt anyone."

Mars flashes me a confident look. "You won't."

I wish I had his certainty.

Shifting nervously on my seat, I can't help fidgeting with the hem of my dress where it rests just below my knees. "I still don't understand what my powers are supposed to be. All I seem to be able to do is kill plants. Maybe I'm not Venus at all more like the Goddess of Death."

Leaning back in his chair insolently, legs slightly apart, his attention roams to the people around us. "You have the power to make people fall in love. Make them fall in love with you. You can bestow beauty on others. Show them how beautiful the world is around them."

"How?" I question softly.

"That's something you have to figure out. Your awakening started back in the church, but it's not complete. I can try and guide you, but our abilities are vastly different."

Mars' mentioning of where I was tortured threatens to drag up memories, but breathing deeply, I manage to press past them.

"So, what? I seduce their hearts and enslave men and women?" I attempt to tease to lighten my mood.

A growl leaves his lips. "You're not seducing or enslaving the males here."

Eyes widening, I don't miss the flash of jealousy, which crosses his face. Arrogant, aloof, he regards me with a regal brooding look. He really does appear divine and untouchable when he's like this: an all bossy, ancient roman male.

The God of War doesn't want me tempting another man's heart. Why does that make me feel all warm on the inside? A small sense of feminine smugness snakes through me.

Biting my lower lip and trying not to let it show, I turn my head to hide my expression.

Could I ensnare his heart? Make Mars mine forever? His one and only.

He genuinely cares for me. I can see that clearly. It's not just sex on his part. What would it take to make him fall in love with me?

The cozy café, where our table sits, is buzzing with customers. Not just the locals, but holidaymakers and day-trippers passing through.

Listening to the chatter, I make out several different languages, not just Italian.

A couple catch my eye.

You can see they're in love. Young, naïve love…..in its first early budding before becoming deeper. An innocent awareness. The shy glances and little touches, each intimate gesture is so ordinary for them, but it's something far more.

Heads together where they sit at a table, in a corner, beside the wall of the café, they speak softly together as if nothing else exists in the world.

The longer I observe the couple, the stronger I feel an energy that spirals up through the layers of my skin. Pure. Radiant. It pulses in time with the thump of my heart.

"You feel it don't you?" Mars' whispered words are in the shell of my ear. He's so close I can smell his familiar scent, which sends carnal hunger roaring up through my body. How can I want him so much? Around him, I'm insatiable.

"They're in love," I murmur and push back the images of our sweat soaked, naked bodies entwined, which are playing through my head.

"The fact you can sense that proves you're Venus, Goddess of Love, but just remember, all powers have a light and dark to them."

Warily, I turn my head to face him. We're inches apart, lips almost touching. This close, I get lost in the depth of his beautiful brown eyes. "What do you mean?"

"Imagine loving someone who doesn't love you back. Binding hearts to follow you blindly with no will of their own. Wars have not just been fought over hatred. Love can be destructive too. You could bring the world to its knees. Wielding what powers you have, is a responsibility. We're here to protect mankind even from ourselves."

Is that what would happen if I succumbed to the dark, I have to wonder? Could I destroy the world with love?

Tilting closer, his mouth touches mine in the sweetest kiss. Gentle, tender, I surrender to it completely.

I'm reluctant to let it end when he pulls away.

Rising, lacing his strong fingers with mine, he helps me to my feet. "Come on, let's take a walk," he suggests with a husky voice.

I'd rather go back to his house and fuck, but I know that's just my out of control libido talking. Mars had mentioned that gods have high sex drives. I guess it applies to goddesses too. I have sex on the brain whenever I'm around him. If I gave into it, I don't think we'd ever leave a bedroom again.

"What are you thinking about?"

"Nothing," I answer him awkwardly, clearing my throat.

The grin he gives me is far too knowing. "Later, my beauty, I'll take you back to bed and fuck you, or anywhere else in my house you desire, but for now, let's enjoy the village."

"Your employees don't know you're a god, right?"

That earns me a look as if I've gone crazy. "Of course not. We don't broadcast what we are. Only a select few know the truth."

"I was just wondering how they rationalize you appearing and disappearing all the time. I mean, they have to notice there's no car..."

Halting, Mars pulls me into his embrace. "Stop worrying. We've been safe for centuries, and it won't change."

Nestling my head on his chest, I savor the way I fit perfectly against him. "I'm not safe from Pluto, though, am I? I can't not worry about that. We can't stay in Tuscany forever. You'll be wanted back in Rome sooner or later. I don't want to stay here without you. Yet, you can't guard me twenty-four seven. You have work to do, and I refuse to be a prisoner for the rest of my life, even if it's for my own protection."

The arms around me tighten so much, for a second, I think he might actually crack my ribs.

"He won't touch you again, Vicky. I swear it to you. He has no idea where you are. Put your mind at ease and let me take care of you."

Instead of answering, I squeeze him back just as tightly.

Mars might have just made me a promise, but even as the God of War, I'm not sure he can keep it. Without powers, I'm vulnerable. Just another regular human who can easily die.

Pluto is searching for me. How I know it? I don't know, but the feeling is growing together with an impending sense of doom.

He failed last time. He had me, but I know in my gut if he takes me again, my end will come quickly. He won't make the mistake of taking things slow.

MARS

Chapter nineteen

I can see Vicky is still getting used to traveling to a different location through space by the way she grips her stomach and shakes her head after we land in England. I know she'll get used to it, though, and celebrate the fact it's so much more comfortable and safer than traveling by plane. Apollo and Hercules land with us and immediately set up sentry duty outside her quintessential English cottage in the middle of the Devon countryside. I shiver at the cold. I've been to England numerous times for one reason or another, and it always rains. I wouldn't say it's my favorite place in the world, although the people are tolerable.

It had taken me a while to convince my father to allow us to come here. When I explained I would use it as part of Vicky's training, he reluctantly agreed. We'd finished our walk in the piazza this morning, spent a few hours in bed, and now as the sun sets on another gloomy day in England, we've arrived here to get as many of Vicky's belonging as we can to make her feel welcome in my villa. Despite her protestations, I've no plans to leave it for the next few weeks. If I had my way, we wouldn't even be leaving my bed, now, but I need to make her feel comfortable.

"I can't believe all that has happened to me since I left here a few days ago. It seems like a dream still." Vicky digs into her pocket for a key and realizes she doesn't have one. It will be with her belongings, which my father has another of my brothers, Mercury, currently obtaining back from the cheap hotel in Rome.

"It probably will for a while." I place my hand on the door, and it magically opens.

"One key for all." She lets out a little chuckle, which warms my heart to hear.

"Our powers give us the protection we need from those who would break and enter. Keys, not so much."

"Good to know." She pushes the door open and steps inside her home. I feel her inhale the scent of familiarity she would get from returning to a place so comforting to her.

"Sorry for the mess." She looks around and bites her lip. I notice the chaos of the room, with clothes discarded from the packing of suitcases strewn on the floor. A bottle of half-drunk wine sits on the table with two glasses. Vicky walks over and picks up one of the glasses. "We had a mini packing party and realized we would be late for the flight so ran out leaving everything as it was. I was going to tidy up when I got home."

The glass turns black in her hands, and I know her emotions are playing with the powers starting to course through her body.

"Damn." She looks up at me with eyes watering. "This was my favorite glass. Can you turn it back?"

I shake my head and step closer to her and take the glass from her hand and put it on the table.

"I can't but you can. You're remembering the sadness of the situation you are in. Remember the happiness instead." I shut my eyes and feel the laughter and excitement of Vicky and Susan as they packed and decided on what they would see first in Rome. The whole house is full of amusement and fun. There's no sadness here. "Feed off the house," I tell her and lead her over to a wall, placing her hand out flat against the whitewashed stone. She looks at me in confusion.

"I don't understand."

"Beauty and love are all around you. You saw today in the piazza, the young couple and the fledgling emotion between them. If we allowed the bad part of our powers to rule over our emotions, then they'd have been fighting. If I allowed it, they probably would have produced guns from their pockets and started a fight to rival those from old country and westerns. But my mind was calm, and I savored the essence of peace. If I became angry, now, this house would quake and collapse around us. Your neighbors would blame you for the situation, and an ensuing legal battle would start. Probably even the cows and sheep in the fields would start a war over who had the better patch of grass. That's why when your mind goes dark you become the Goddess of Destruction to flora and fauna rather than the Goddess of Beauty. Plants have always been more symbolic of our emotions than more modern creations. When you meet her, please don't ever say I told you this, but if my aunt Ceres is having a bad time of the month, then you can guarantee a famine of sorts will be reported somewhere in the world."

"Ceres?" Vicky interrupts, and I make a mental note I

need to provide her with a list of the discovered gods and goddesses and what they rule.

"Yes, she's the Goddess of Agriculture. Not the best thing to be when you're in a bad mood. But on a good day, she can create some stunning displays and enough food to feed even the poorest villages for years."

"I'd like to meet her. Maybe she can help repair your vineyards I destroyed."

I chuckle, "I believe you'll do that yourself soon. But for now, let's concentrate on the glass. Remember something happy associated with it."

Vicky bites her lip as she looks toward the glass but still keeps her hand splayed on the beauty of the house.

"I don't think I can." Her body deflates, and I know she remembers the sadness of Susan's death.

I suck in a breath as I think.

"Who gave you the glass?"

"Susan."

"Why?"

"It was when I moved in here."

"A housewarming gift?"

"Yes, in my old place, we used plastic glasses to drink our wine from because I wanted all new for a fresh start. I'd seen it for sale and knew I had to have it. My parents died a few years ago and left me enough money to buy it outright. It wasn't in the best condition, so I was able to get a loan to make some repairs. When I moved in, she came around the first night and brought a bottle of champagne and the glasses. She'd found them for sale in an antique shop, and they matched the house beautifully. We sat in front of the fire, talking and drinking until the early hours. We had boxes all around us, but it just seemed more important to enjoy the feeling of the house."

I could sense the emotions emanating off Vicky as she spoke. They twisted in my gut, and I had to suppress my own feelings because anger surfaced at what Pluto and Marco had done to Susan. I'd seen her body. I knew how much she'd suffered in her final moments. I'd felt Vicky's pain surge through my body as she experienced the same. Marco had died painfully, and Pluto would suffer the same consequences, or as far as I could inflict them on him. He may be immortal as a god, but I'll make sure he's left with nothing and bound to his own hell in the underworld.

I looked at where my hand covered Vicky's on the wall. Black oozed from underneath our combined skin.

"Vicky. You must remember it with happiness."

"How? They killed her. My best friend. The only person to have been there for me through so much."

I tried not to let the remark sting, given I'd rescued her.

"Memories. You have to remember the ones, which make you happy and smile. You can't allow the darkness of what happened to claim you. That glass is special; it was given to you by a friend who loved you. She wanted to do something nice for you. This house, it's a legacy of your parents. I didn't know them, or your relationship with them, but I can sense from the pictures you have of them you loved them. Remember Susan for the friendship you had."

Tears start to stream down Vicky's cheeks.

"It's too hard; I'm too raw."

"And it won't get any easier if you allow the darkness of your emotions to consume you."

"I can't."

"Try, please," I plead.

She shuts her eyes and silences for a few moments. The blackness still spreads over the wall.

"I remember something," she blurts out, suddenly, and opens her eyes. "I remember a shopping trip. I don't think I've ever laughed so much. We were looking at fancy outfits for a party. We tried on so many different things: cowgirls, aliens, vampires, even a Roman Goddess. We both finally decided on sixties outfits. We decorated our faces with 'ban the bomb' signs and flowers. It was so much fun."

The tears in her eyes start to dry up, and a small smile spreads across her face.

"No, that wasn't it. That wasn't the funniest time. She went out on a date with this guy, a blind date, and the guy actually brought his mum with him. I laughed so hard my stomach ached, when she told me."

I look at the wall, and I notice the blackness has receded. The whitewash of the wall is back and sparkling in newness. It seems like she's just decorated the room.

I pull her hand from the wall and lead her across to the glass as she starts another story.

"We tried dog sitting once. This crazy lady had four poodles. We took them out for a walk, and it was just chaos. By the time we got back, I'm not sure who was covered in more mud, the dogs or us. Needless to say, we didn't walk any more dogs."

I place Vicky's hand on the glass, and instantly, the marring on it starts to disappear. She gasps.

"It's fixed."

"Emotions, happiness in your heart caused it to revert back to its beauty. You have to remember the good times, not the sadness."

She looks around the room and notices a vase of flowers past their best.

"I pick flowers once a week from the garden. I love all the different colors out there. The garden was already designed when I moved in. The people who lived here before preferred gardening to the house. I try to maintain it as best as I can."

She reaches out and touches the flowers, which droop and hang forlornly in the vase. Nothing happens at first, but gradually, the petals brighten in color and flutter back to a glorious state.

"I did it," she stutters breathlessly. "I didn't kill a plant. I brought it back to life."

"You brought it back to beauty." I bring her into my arms and kiss the top of her head.

"I can be this goddess, can't I?" she utters into my chest.

"You've been her all along. You just needed to unlock your belief."

She steps up onto her tiptoes and kisses my lips. My cock instantly goes hard. I've always been insatiable when it comes to sex, but around Vicky, my Venus, I want inside her twenty- four seven.

"Why don't we look at packing some of your belongings and taking them back to Tuscany, and then we can work on some more of your powers. What do you say?"

She bites her lip. "I think maybe we should have a little fun in my bed first. I need happier memories." She winks at me and drops her hand. I take it and follow her to the bedroom.

VENUS
Chapter twenty

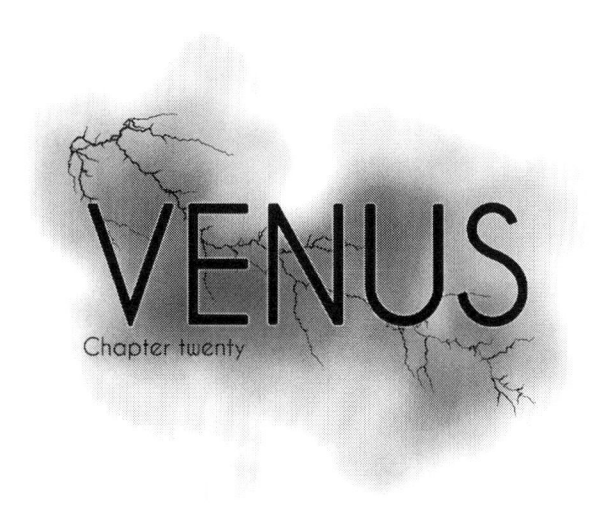

Humming to myself softly, I stretch under the warmth of the afternoon sun. Around me, I can hear the sounds of the birds. Nestled between two rows, not far from the house, I'm hidden from prying eyes. Handy when you want to sunbathe topless.

Seven days since my traumatic experience and the loss of Susan, I've found a slither of peace.

Mars and I have settled into an easy flow. Mornings spent lazing around in bed, having sex. Even that has evolved. It's not all wild desperation, now. Our passion changes like the wind. Sometimes it's hard and rough, other times tender and gentle. He's a man who can easily make me beg and other times have me crying with laughter.

We have lunch in the villages around Tuscany. He's so keen on showing his country. He's so passionate about his culture.

Some afternoons, I draw in the studio he arranged to

have put together while we were collecting some of my things from England. The surprise reduced me to tears.

With Mars' encouragement and enthusiasm, I started sketching a scene from the vineyard, that same day. I hadn't realized how much I needed it until my pencil touched the paper, and I felt myself immerse in creativity. When things had clicked in place, I'd been lost in my own little world. Watching the scenery take form in the sketch book had lifted my spirits.

With everything Pluto and Mario took from me, they hadn't stolen this.

The only darkness to over shadow the last few days was Susan's funeral. Somehow Mars was able to cut through the red tape and have her body transported home. Her parents had been devastated already bearing the news from the Italian authorizes. The questions had been endless. I'd only been able to tell them a thin layer of the truth. If I'd spoken of Gods and Goddess, they would have thought me mad. Mars had been at my side the entire time. His support had meant everything to me as I'd broken down in tears and anguish. Saying goodbye to my best friend as they'd lowered her into the ground had been the hardest thing I've ever done.

Scooping up my bikini top, I slip it back on to cover my breasts. Even I know the dangers of the Italian sun. Skin as pale as mine can burn easily. Small doses, as I've been doing every day, and I'm already gaining a tan. It'll never be the golden brown of Mars' Mediterranean heritage, but at least, I look more like I fit in.

Rising from the sunbed, the dry earth is hot beneath my bare soles.

Glancing towards the house, I know it's empty.

Mars isn't back yet. I don't know how I know, but it's becoming easier to sense his presence whenever he's near. I guess it's part of my goddess powers. Or maybe it's our connection?

The longer I'm around him, the more I feel a bond. As if we're meant to be together. As if this time with each other is meant to be.

"Have you seen Mars?"

The question startles me, sending my heart leaping up into my throat. Apart from Luigi, Mars' son, we haven't seen anyone else.

Turning, I find a woman, her dark eyes watching me with dislike. I know who she is straight away. Bellona the mother of Mars' son.

We might not have met, but I've heard her description from both males in her life. What they have told me pales in comparison. She's more than beautiful. Just like Mars, she's blessed with the allure and sensuality of Mediterranean features. Tall, slender, I could see her easily gracing a catwalk in Paris or Milan.

"No, he was checking things up at the main building," I inform her, lacing the fingers of both hands together in front of my bikini clad body. "His manager had papers for him to fill out, and he had a meeting, but he said he wouldn't be long."

I'm fully aware of her critical, sweeping gaze. It's a little catty, made to make me feel less in comparison. I've been on the receiving end of looks like that before.

"I'll come back to the house and wait for him there, then," Bellona replies stiffly.

Biting my tongue, I hold in my defensive response. "Sure,

I was just going back for something cool to drink. I'd be happy for you to join me."

A jerk of her head in agreement and she moves off without me toward the waiting building.

Trailing after her, I take my time.

I can't blame her for not liking me. Before I arrived, she and Mars still had a thing. A relationship I know, from what he told me, he ended the moment he met me. Even if she took it well, as he claimed, she obviously didn't show him the pain it caused. It's there in the depths of her lovely eyes. Bitterness at being discarded.

That has to be so much worse as an immortal. I'm not talking about a matter of years. For them, it's centuries. How many emotions build for someone over such a long period of time?

I'm sure it doesn't help Luigi seems to be spending all his spare time with us, too. The boy has taken to constantly being at my side. I have no idea if Mars asked him to keep an eye on me, or maybe like his father, he feels responsible for the woman staying on their land.

A frown creases my brow as I realize I haven't seen him today.

"Is it something I could help you with?" I offer as we reach the sanctuary of the shade, stepping into the cool exterior of the house. Thank god, Mars has air conditioning. Some of the days become unbearably hot.

Bellona glances around the room.

I know she's taking in the changes. Many of my things and artwork have been spread around my temporary new home. Strangely, they look right among Mars' possessions. Something he commented on the other night. It surprised me he sounded so happy about it.

"No." The one word is clipped and sharp.

Taking two glasses down from a cupboard, I pull open the fridge and grab the bottle of natural still water. It's deliciously cold within my hand. Licking my dry lips, it makes me realize just how thirsty sunbathing has made me.

Sliding onto the chair next to the wooden kitchen table, Bellona accepts the glass I offer her.

"Where's Luigi today?" I ask, hoping conversation regarding her son might ease some of the animosity.

Pouring my own drink, I screw the bottle shut and slip it back onto its shelf within the fridge before banging it closed.

"With his tutor."

"He's a very bright and clever boy. You should be very proud of him."

Lifting the glass, she sips at the contents, observing me over the rim with distrust and something else I can't quite put my finger on.

Nervously tucking loose stands of my blonde hair behind my ears, I take the seat opposite her.

I hope Mars won't be long. This isn't how I imagined meeting the woman he shares a child with. In fact, I've been dreading it. Doing it alone makes it a hundred times worse.

Gulping down some water, I avoid her stare.

"I would do anything for my son." Her quiet voice breaks the awkward silence that's been stretching. "Whatever it takes to keep him safe and happy. Remove any threat if necessary. You understand?"

"I'm not a threat, Bellona. I'd never do anything to harm Luigi or his Father."

"You already do."

I frown at the accusation, an unseen chill creeping through my body. "What do you mean?"

Raking a hand through her long mane of black hair, she turns her head to stare at the view beyond the window. "Tuscany has always been a safe place for me and my family, away from Rome and the others there. You've brought attention to this place. It's only a matter of time before they come for you."

The thought of Luigi in danger makes my heart twist. Unlike his parents, he's only beginning to understand his powers. In a way, we're alike in that respect. Both still growing. If Pluto came for me, would he take the boy, too? His agenda is so corrupt. Wouldn't taking Mars' son be the perfect revenge? Turning the boy against him?

"But they haven't found me, so far. I have to believe eventually they'll give up looking for me. With so many forgotten gods and goddesses to find, why just focus on me forever?" I tell her, hoping I sound more convincing than I feel.

Mars is so adamant this place is safe. Yet, with all the powers these gods and goddesses possess, they don't have the ability to track me down?

A smile flits across Bellona's lips. "You sound like Mars."

"I think all his positivity is rubbing off on me. To be honest, after what happened, I really need it." Staring down into my empty glass, sadness dances around the edges of my good mood. "He's shown me if I let what happened rule me, then it means Pluto and Mario have won. That I give them exactly what they want. With the things I can do as the Goddess of Love, I can't afford to let that happen. The thought of hurting others makes me feel sick. I want to use what I can do for good. Bring love to the world."

"You're a brave woman, and I am sorry for everything you have been through. Even though I doubt we'll ever be friends, I want you to know that."

Meeting her watchful eyes, I reach over the table to touch her hand. "I'm sorry for taking Mars away from you."

I don't want to be the cause of pain. Love turned sour is something I can sense churning inside her. Mars may not have loved her, but that didn't stop her falling for the God of War.

Her fingers squeeze mine in acceptance. "Men are blind fools, and I was stupid to think things between us were more than physical even when I birthed Luigi. I gave him a son, and he still didn't want me as I wanted him."

"I'm so sorry."

"It was destined he'd find his opposite. I was never meant to be that woman."

Her words give me a little rush of hope. Mars and I still haven't spoken about feelings. Sex doesn't always involve them. I learned that in the past, but the way we fuck, there's more than something carnal behind it. Of that I am now certain.

"But that doesn't mean you won't find the man who's meant to love you," I encourage, my voice soft.

"Have you told him how you feel?" she asks, slipping her hand from mine and withdrawing from the comfort.

Heat warms my cheeks. Am I really that obvious? "No, I haven't told Mars I love him."

In one quick move, Bellona drains the contents of her glass. "It's probably for the best."

The swift hardness in her voice confuses me.

Before I can blink, she's behind me. A forearm presses against my windpipe, choking. The other snatches one of my arms up and pins it painfully up on my back.

"What are you doing?" I manage to gasp as I am dragged up off my chair.

"What needs to be done. I told you, Vicky, when it comes to my family, I'll go to any lengths to protect them."

My struggles are overpowered, and it's terrifying–the strength I can feel flowing through her tall slender body.

Goosebumps ripple over my skin as energy builds around us. It's one I'm still getting used to. In a flash, she teleports us.

Blinking rapidly, my eyes adjust to the change. Gone is the peace and harmony of Mars' Tuscan home. Around us now is an office. Stylish, chic, there's an air of coldness and clinical cleanliness screaming at something unnatural.

Shoved forward, I all but stumble. My knees connect with a sofa, stopping me from tumbling to the floor.

"There," Bellona growls behind me. "I've given you what you want. Now, you return my son to me."

Head jerking up, my shocked expression morphs in to terror.

There sitting on the ledge of a desk, one long leg crossed over the other, is Pluto. Evil smirk pinned over his face, his sinister dark eyes bore into mine.

"Nice of you to join me, Vicky. Our time together was so short last time we met. A mistake I intend to make sure is corrected this time. We'll get to know each other so much better, and perhaps, we'll explore your growing powers as well as other things we didn't get to enjoy."

I've lost my voice. Seeing him up close again, so soon, sends primitive panic through my system. He's evil. Love doesn't exist in his being. That's something I can see clearly, now. Darkness is all I sense. No hint of light. Nothing softer.

His attention rakes over my half naked form. The skin he can see on display from my barely there bikini.

I want to run. Scream. Curl into a protective ball, but instead, I remain rooted to the spot frozen.

"Pluto. Where is my boy?" Bellona's screeches. In three swift steps, she's across the room, a hostile whirlwind of anger and rage.

Tilting his head, the God of the Underworld regards the female with a look of dismissal. "You'll get him back all in good time. For now, I need you to distract Mars."

"That wasn't the deal we made when you snatched Luigi."

"Things change, Bellona. You should know that." He grins. His taunt meant to hurt. "Now go, before he gets back and figures things out."

Her eyes narrow. "You've already proven I can't trust you."

"The child is still breathing. You should be grateful, and if you wish him to continue doing so, you'll do as you're told."

Bellona flashes me a look of defeat and regret.

I can't hate her. Even though she's betrayed me, she was doing it to save Luigi. She loves her child with all her heart.

She vanishes, leaving me alone with a male I prayed never to meet again.

Rising from his position, Pluto strolls, bridging the distance between us with a menace, which sends my heart racing harder.

"Who do you think Mars will choose when it comes down to you or his son?"

"Luigi," I answer him with certainty.

Mars is fiercely protective of him. I've seen his pride shining through. I'd never expect him to sacrifice his child over me.

"I beg to differ. He'll agonize over the choice he'll have to make. Something, which will haunt him for the rest of his existence and make him even darker. Perhaps unhinged? I do hope so. I want war unleashed and unhindered on the world."

Backing up, I keep my attention on him until a wall prevents me from escaping any further.

Why haven't I gained my teleportation powers yet? It's something, which would've helped, right now.

His expression is knowing. He's enjoying seeing how frightened he makes me feel. Revels in it as if it's his choice of drug.

Coming to a stop, Pluto barely leaves any space between us.

I flinch as he reaches out, coiling a strand of my blonde hair around one thick long finger before tugging on it painfully. "I've been looking forward to this. You may have escaped me before, but this time, you won't be so lucky. Now, let's see how destructive the power of love can really be."

MARS

Chapter twenty-one

"We've been far too lenient on him in the past. Pluto's running rings around us. He's risking exposure on a daily basis, and it draws more and more people down into his world. We need to put a stop to it." I bang my fist on the desk in front of me, and my father raises a questioning eyebrow at me.

"Is this your brain or your heart speaking?" he replies, and Apollo chuckles. I turn and give my brother a glare so forceful he instantly silences.

"Both." I snap my attention back to my father and bite out. "I'm sick of being one step behind him. Mario was a sick man, and Pluto allowed him to flourish under his authority. I spent ages looking through the files of evidence. It's forever scarred into my brain. Are we just going to sit around and wait for the next Mario to present himself to Pluto, or are we going to do something about the God of the Underworld?"

"I wish it were that simple, my son." My father pushes back the heavy oak chair he's sitting on and stands. "Pluto's intrinsically linked with all the gods, just as I am. We are all symbiotic with each other. I'm not sure how much we're going to be able to stop him."

"We can bind him in some way. Destroy his business, run it into the ground, and force him to the Underworld. The longer he's on Earth, the more trouble he's causing." My temper's rising. I'd spent the morning dealing with business at my estates in Tuscany, and then my father called me here for this crisis meeting. I'm sick of discussing how we'll proceed when it comes to Pluto. I want his head on a platter, preferably stuffed with my favorite fruit.

"Mars, you must be sensible."

"I'm done with that," I groan with frustration. "I want blood."

"That's the war inside you talking."

"No"–I interrupt my father and bang my fists on the table again– "it's the person who's had to put a goddess back together who's talking. I've had to watch her nearly destroy herself every time a flower has wilted from her emotions."

"How is she dealing with her emerging powers?" My father changes the subject and asks.

"Well…" I'll not be distracted though. "Pluto uses illegal activities to generate funds. Let's hit him where it hurts. Let's cut off those funds. His drug shipments hit Naples once a month. That day is soon. Let's bust him and have them taken away. He won't be able to sell them, and he'll have to concentrate on generating funds elsewhere. It'll distract him from the fight for the gods, albeit for a short period of time, but enough to allow us to retrieve and secure more before he discovers them."

Hercules steps up to the desk from where he's been quietly watching in the corner of the room.

"Father, I'm actually inclined to agree with Mars. We've been sitting back for far too long now, waiting for Pluto's next move. I know it has been because of the fear of harm coming to the humans, but I have to say if they're involved willingly in drug smuggling, they deserve all that's coming to them."

"Apollo?" my father questions my other brother.

"I don't think it would hurt to take the fight to him for once."

My father sits back in his chair, his whole demeanor weary and full of defeat.

"I was wrong to ever think a time of peace would exist again for the gods. Too much has happened, and too much hatred exists. When we mix that with the ever-expanding human elements, I think a pre-emptive strike is our best course of action."

I reach out over the mountain of files on his desk, all full of cases that'll be god related.

"I wish nothing more than peace, especially with Vicky in my life."

Hercules chuckles.

"I never thought I'd see the day my brother would want to stay home and have sex with the same woman."

"Shut it," I retort and hold a fist up.

"Happens to the best of us." My father lets out a long breath and smirks. "You'd better get back to her. I'm going to go see your mother. Hercules, Apollo, you can make the necessary plans. Find out when the shipment is due, and we'll put a stop to it."

My brothers and I shudder at the thought of what he'll be doing with my mother in a few minutes.

"Well, brothers, father has spoken. You better get on with

your work." With a purposeful show, I grab my crotch and give it a tug. "I have instructions to go make Vicky happy." I leave the room to the sounds of them groaning.

I reappear in my lounge in Tuscany.

"Vicky?" I call and head toward the kitchen for a drink. Two half empty glasses sit upon the table. Strange, I muse and pour myself some water into a clean glass I retrieve from the cupboard. "Luigi?"

My son has spent more time at our place, recently, than the home he shares with his mother. He's taken a real liking to Vicky, and I love to watch it. Although, if he's here now, he's being sent home. I need my cock to be buried deeply inside Vicky's succulent pussy and hearing her scream my name over and over again. My son being here doesn't really allow for that, no matter how much I adore him.

I finish my water, scoop up the other two glasses, and deposit them in the sink for washing later. A floral feminine scent fills the room, but I know instantly, without even looking, it's not Vicky.

"Bellona," I huff out with frustration and turn to face her where she stands in the doorway. She's dressed in only a silk gown, which leaves little to the imagination with its gossamer transparency. Leaning back against the kitchen cupboards, I cross my feet at the ankles and fold my arms across my chest. "I think you better turn straight around and leave."

"Why?" She runs her tongue slowly over her lips. Once upon a time, I would have found it sexy. In fact, I'm pretty certain it's the reason she got pregnant in the first place, but right now, it irritates me and makes my skin crawl.

"Because whatever game you're playing isn't going to happen."

"Why not?" She saunters towards me, seductively swaying her hips. Her tiny hand is placed in the center of my chest, but there's no warmth coming from it, only chills so cold my body shudders.

"I love, Vicky," I reply adamantly.

"She's not worthy of you. She's weak and will never be able to cater to all your needs. Only I know the darkness running through your head because it's there in mine, too. We both will never see the world as others do because we have the power to destroy it with one angry word." She leans forward to kiss my chest through the casual t-shirt I'm wearing. I push her back.

"No, and I'm warning you. If you don't leave, this second, and allow me to find Vicky, then it'll be your world that's destroyed. I'd never want to upset my son, but if you can't behave with at least a little decorum, then I think I may have to reconsider you being in his life." I bend down low so I'm in her face. I'm not a nice man when it's called for, and the next words I speak are designed to cause as much pain as possible to my former consort. "Maybe I'll have him call Vicky his mother."

The gasp she makes causes the room to shake.

"No." A single tear drops down her cheek. Bellona doesn't cry…. she's a Goddess of War. I place my finger in the tear, and the force of the emotion behind it takes my breath away. I double over, clutching my chest as pain so fervent starts to rip through it. I'm gasping for air as the feelings running through Bellona's mind cascade through my body in a torrent so fierce my head is left spinning.

"Luigi!" I cry out.

Her bottom lip quivers.

"I didn't have a choice."

"Choice?" Her words suddenly hit me like a ton of bricks. "Vicky? Where is she?"

"He promised me he'd give him back. He's all I have, Mars. He's my world. He's what keeps me grounded and stops me from starting the wars you fight so hard to prevent. I can't lose him. I can't? Please."

Without thinking, I grip her around the neck and pin her up against the wall. Her eyes go wide as saucers as she registers the shock of my actions.

"What did you do?" I growl out with so much fury a storm erupts outside the villa. Rain descends in a powerful downpour, which blankets the world from view. Thunder booms out its loud call of anger while the lightning erupts from the sky in a potent flame.

"I had no choice."

"Tell me," I shout, and the wall behind her crumbles into smithereens on the floor. My house rocks, the earth itself shaking from a quake so powerful a line to hell itself rips open through my kitchen floor.

"Pluto said I would get Luigi back if I brought Vicky to him. Please, Mars. He lied. He still has our son, and he's going to kill him. You have to stop him."

I drop her to the floor as the words slowly register into my head. I've lost Vicky, again, but this time, my son has gone with her. Pluto has the two people in his hands who mean the world to me. I would die for them. I can feel that I'm broken. He's won. I take one final look at Bellona who lays, a sniveling mess, on the floor.

"Run, hide because this ends now. You've wanted a war my Goddess, by fuck, you're going to get one."

I turn and look at the jagged hole that's shattered the marble perfection of my home. I stride over to it and call for my spear. It instantly appears in my hand. My eyes shut, and the clothes of mankind I wear disappear, the ancient Roman livery replacing them a symbol of my strength and fury.

"When Luigi returns, get him as far away from here as possible. Rome, Italy, our world will fall today."

I shuffle my foot closer to the edge of the hole. The earth's core burns from within, but I don't feel its heat, for my own exceeds anything a puny planet can throw at me, now. I don't shy away from it. I don't feel anything, not even when I jump into the hole and descend into the Underworld.

VENUS
Chapter twenty-two

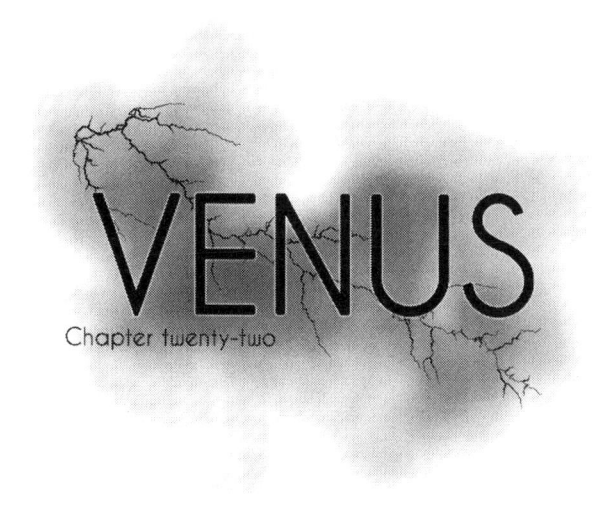

Pluto groans, his panting breath searing my ear. As he shudders over me, I feel his cock pulse as he fills me with his cum. The burn of his seed makes me convulse in pain. Pinned as I am with his weight, there's no escape.

Biting the inside of my cheek until I taste blood, I refuse to let him hear me cry. Eyes screwed shut, the tears burn behind me eyelids.

I fought hard to stop him. Refused to go quietly, but, still he overpowered me. With his inhuman strength, I never stood a chance.

The cold marble surface of his desk pressed against my thighs and torso grounding me to the defilement I've just had to endure.

"I can see why Mars enjoys your cunt so much," he mutters in my ear, thrusting lazily into me a few more times. "It really is divine in every sense of the word."

I wince as his softening cock pulls out of me.

My head's still spinning from his ferocity. The bikini I'm

wearing barely a barrier against his attack. It was so fast there was no time to brace for what was to come. All he had to do was hook the scrap of material to one side to take me.

Peeling myself off his desk, my legs shake weakly. I'm fully aware of his cum trickling down the inside of my thighs.

The darkness Mars had kept at bay the last week simmers to the surface. Just beneath my skin, it seethes.

Pluto is a monster.

Turning slowly, I confront the Devil himself.

Raised, still bleeding, his cheek bares the claw marks from where I attempted to defend myself.

"You look so beautiful tainted and wearing the marks of my possession." He smirks. Reaching for his crotch, he zips up his trousers.

"You've got me, taken what you wanted. Now, let Luigi go," I reply, my voice a rough whisper. I hate him and wish I had the power to make him burn.

"And lose a bargaining chip? I don't think so."

"Mars will come for him no matter what. He'll destroy you."

Pluto chuckles. "Oh, I'm counting on him coming, but he won't hurt me, not if he wants to see his son again. No, the God of War will become my pawn."

When he takes a step closer, I can't stop my instinctive reaction to flinch back.

"You're weak and pathetic, Vicky. Look at yourself– The Goddess of Love?" With calculating paces, he crowds me. "I've fucked you against your will. Let my pet psychopath kill your friend and hurt you. Does that invoke love inside you or a thirst for revenge?"

Lips pressed together, I clench my teeth.

He's right. What I feel is anything but love. Rage. An insidious need to strike out so he experiences the same raw harsh emotions and sensations he's given me.

"Embrace the hate. Let it fill you. You'll be so much stronger when you do."

Meeting his eyes, I shake my head. "I'm not going to give you what you want."

"Oh, you will, in time. Something I have plenty of. I intend to keep on enjoying you. As concubines go, I think you'll keep my attention for a very long time before I get bored." Snatching a fistful of my hair, Pluto drags me up against the length of his chest. Cock hardening in the front of his trousers, it prods my stomach through the coarseness of the material.

Twisting my head, I try to avoid his lips, but his teeth sink into my bottom lip, holding me in place.

Everything inside me screams out in loathing.

Hand gripping the back of my skull, he keeps me in place as he devours my mouth.

I want it to be over. He's so fucking repellent it makes me want to gag. To wash his taste and scent off me forever.

Palms pressed against his shirt front, somehow, I find the strength to shove him away.

Pluto grins, rubbing the pad of his thumb along his jaw as he watches my expression of disgust.

That one gesture is enough to make me snap.

He thinks he can get away with it all. Degrade me. Rape. Bring the world into chaos and Mars to his knees. Whatever he does to me, I won't let him hurt the man I love. Somehow, I'll find Luigi and get us free.

Lunging for him, I go for his face with a scream rising

straight from my soul. Fingers connect with soft flesh. I drive them deeply, scoring my nails into his skin.

Pluto hisses.

A backhanded blow sends me to my knees. Cheek on fire from the punch, it leaves me with the taste of blood on my tongue.

"I like your fire but not your claws. With Mario dead, I had to find another torturer, and I think my new apprentice is fitting for the task."

Yanking me up by my hair, he drags me forcefully across the floor.

Clutching his wrist, a scream leaves my throat the agony blinding. He's going to leave me to one of his minions. Have me tortured again while he looks on? Panic fractures inside me, and I know I won't be able to live through this a second time.

Writhing, twisting, I can't break free as my bare feet scape against the unyielding hardness of the cold stone floor.

The sound of a metal door opening registers. A second later, I'm drawn upward and slammed back into a chair.

Arms captured, they're pinned to my sides.

Giving me an unfriendly leer, the two males restraining me click the cuffs into place, preventing me from moving.

"Let me up, you son of a bitch. I'm going to kill you myself."

Clucking his tongue, Pluto dabs with a handkerchief at the fresh damage I've left in red, long scratches on his arrogant face. "Such pretty, empty threats. You're in my domain, now. The Underworld. There's nothing you can do to harm me permanently here. You're barely a toddler in terms of a goddess. Still unsure of your powers. Still not fully awakened."

Jutting my chin out, I spare him a glare. "Oh. trust me, you're going to be screwed when they do."

Smirk creeping up his lips, he nods at one of the guards.

Stalking to the door, the male returns a second later, but he's not alone.

Luigi.

Pale, shaken, Mars' son can't hide his look of terror as he spots the God of the Underworld hovering in the corner.

"Come here, boy." Crooking his finger, Pluto beckons him closer.

Hesitation dances over the young boy's handsome features.

I'm more than sure Bellona and Mars must have warned him about this monster.

Pluto huffs in annoyance. It's obvious he doesn't like being disobeyed.

"Luigi. I don't have much patience. If you don't wish to change places with your father's whore, here, then do as you're told."

The words jolt the child from his frozen stare. Eyes rounding further, he finally becomes aware of my presence. "Vicky?"

I'm thankful to still be wearing my bikini. In his hurry to have me, Pluto at least spared me from being naked in front of the boy.

"It's going to be ok," I tell him, praying it won't be a lie.

Stalking forward, Pluto takes Luigi by the scruff of the neck. "No talking and wasting time," he mutters as they come level with a table. Unrolling a cloth, he uncovers a collection of knives hidden beneath. "Alessandro and Salvo are going to teach you to use these."

Breath stuttering helplessly in my lungs, my attention bounces to the two silent men.

No.

Things click into place. Pluto intends to have Mars' son as his next killer. Disbelief threatens to choke me before it slips into rage. How could he plan to destroy his innocence? It's evil. Vile.

"No." Fury laces my tone. "You can't do that to him."

Nervously Luigi glances my way. "I can't. Won't hurt my friend."

"Then, you replace her in the chair," Pluto informs the boy with such icy assurance I have no doubt he intends to see it through if Luigi continues to refuse.

I'm trapped between a need to protect Luigi and prevent the pain I know awaits me. Closing my eyes, I call on my resolve. Can I bare this again, or will it finally break me?

"It's ok.," I tell the child, my smile weak.

"But, Vicky…"

"No. Luigi, I'd never forgive myself." Sitting a little taller, I try not to let him see my fright as I open my eyes. "You're a brave boy, but I couldn't let you do that to save me."

Choosing a blade, Pluto presses it into the boy's hand. "I don't want her permanently damaged. Teach him the places to inflict the most pain," he tells his watching men. "Make sure she experiences plenty of agony, just don't touch her face." He guides the smaller hand that he's holding forward, driving the tip of the weapon through the skin of my shoulder.

Luigi tries desperately to jerk away but lacks the strength.

Muscles tensing, a scream rips from my throat as the metal is dragged along, cutting as it goes.

"Now, if you'll excuse me, I'm expecting your father to

turn up." Releasing his hold, Pluto pushes the boy aside, finally done with his tormenting. "Your mother, I am sure, has let slip exactly where you are. It was expected. While he loses his temper, I intend to use both of you to my advantage."

Handing one of the guards the knife, he straightens his suit jacket before strolling from the room.

Glancing down shakily, I watch the blood flow down from the wound he's left. I know it's only the beginning. One moment in the nightmarish hours I face ahead of me.

MARS
Chapter twenty-three

"Welcome Mars, please take a seat. Would you care for a drink?" Pluto knows I'm there before I even have a chance to thrust my spear through his chest. Proserpina, his forced consort, stands next to the dark-haired figure of my uncle. Her eyes are sunken, and I know she mourns the loss of her freedom from the surface. She still has many long months of winter, down here, to endure. I tip my chin toward her to leave. She looks down at Pluto, who nonchalantly waves her away.

"I want them back now!"

"I wasn't aware this was a fancy-dress party." Pluto looks at my clothing, the outfit of a gladiator ready to do battle for what is his.

"I'm reminding you of the strength I possess. Enough games." I point my spear directly at his chest and start to put my weight behind it. "This is a battle you won't win. I'll see to that."

"You're so boring and predictable, Mars. Just like your

father." Pluto clicks his fingers, and my spear is sent flying across the space to embed in the rock formations that adorn the room. "I'm glad your son is different. He has a darkness about him. It must be from his whore of a mother. She really will open her legs for anyone of us. I'm surprised you've allowed him to stay with her. She's faithless to all, except her own cause, and that's power."

"I didn't come here for a boring lecture. I came here for my son and Vicky." I turn and start to walk away from him. "It seems I'll have to tear the underworld apart to find them. Mind you, with a click of my fingers, I can have the underworld destroy itself. War doesn't only apply to the humans. It's everywhere."

"But you can't control those with no souls. They're already dead or indebted to me, so a war with them is inconsequential."

I twist back to my uncle and send a blast of energy so powerful, directly at him, I know when it hits little will be left of the demonic monster who plagues me. It doesn't hit, though, for Orcus appears and diverts it through a wall in a burning explosion of rock and lava.

"Stop wasting your energy and my time." Pluto bangs his hand hard on his desk. "Every moment you continue with your false belief that I'll just hand over my two prized possessions, you allow another part of both of them to die." He smirks. "Not that I doubt there's much beauty left in Venus after I marked her as my own." I'm transfixed with the fury cascading through my veins. My blood is boiling to the point my body will explode. Pluto runs his tongue over his teeth. "I bet she still feels me inside her, my cum still drying between her legs, but that'll be nothing compared to what your son's doing to her. Beauty is only skin deep, and by the time Luigi has finished with her, Venus will have little skin left, which isn't sliced away from her body. Don't you sense it, Mars, the darkness prevailing here in the Underworld? It's growing. I'm going to welcome two new members to my team. Your son's a natural; I feel it in my bones. He's born with a darkness only two parents who control war could give him. He'll be strong–he'll be powerful. He'll be mine, unless you give me what I want."

I allow my mind to connect to Vicky and my son. I can feel the agony the woman I love is in. Her mind, no matter how hard she fights, is losing its ability to see any beauty in the world. She'll be Pluto's soon; I know it. And my son, he's terrified, doing spiteful things to a woman he respects and worships because he has no choice. He's so young he doesn't understand his ability to fight. I've done that to him by protecting him from what the world can be. I've caused him to see only good when in reality evil is around every corner and is stronger than rightness will ever be.

My rage explodes, and ball after ball of energy is sent flying toward Pluto and Orcus. They're deflected, and the room burns brightly with the after effects of my inability to control my emotions. I want Pluto dead–I want the whole fucking world dead. I just want Vicky and Luigi safe. I send another burst of fury, and this time, it rebounds and strikes me on the chest plate. It knocks the breath out of my body, and I collapse to the floor, gasping for air.

"Feeble, weak. You're no God of War." Pluto stalks toward me. "You allow humans to live in peace. They shouldn't even be here on this planet. We should be allowed the freedom we had in the years of old. The darkness needs to take over again and rule as it did then."

"Never!" I shout and push myself back up.

"It's time you listen to me. Vicky will die before the sun sets in Rome unless you submit to me. Luigi will join my forces as my chief torturer. He'll be what Marco was: depraved, savage, all the things you hate. He'll no longer be yours. You have a choice." Pluto expels his own powerful blasts of energy toward me, and I'm sent flying across the room. Allow war to rule."

"Never."

"Allow your emotions to cloud everything, not just here in Rome, but all over the world. Let a chorus of battle cries echo through every street, in every country, in the world. Let human kill human over nothing more than a piece of bread. Allow Armageddon to sweep its way through the human race, so I may emerge a victorious ruler.

"Never," I choke out as Pluto's eyes grow wider and wider with the thought of undefeatable power he can possess with my help. "I'll never destroy the world."

Pluto turns to Orcus.

"Bring him."

I lose control of my own body. I don't know what power allows this to happen, but I follow behind Pluto as he leaves the now decimated room we were in and strides purposefully through the corridors of the underworld. I hear eerie screams and bloodcurdling shouts, calling out from everywhere around me. Wailing moans cause me to shiver. I try to shut my mind to the suffering that's threatening to erupt from continuing down the path I am.

Pluto pushes a door open, and inside, I see Luigi with two men. They're forcing him to push a knife into the stomach of a woman strapped to a chair. She's wearing only a bikini, and I know instantly it's Vicky. She looks up toward me, her eyes black and un-life like. Blood and cuts mar her beautiful skin, but it's the sound of weeping in the room, which causes my heart to tear itself in two. My son, my little boy, cries because he's the one doing these things to her. My body's given its own free governance over movement again, but I've no longer got any fight left in me. I allow my centurion outfit to vanish, and the clothes of a regular human male to appear again. A t-shirt and jeans paired with sandals. Simple, nothing with any bravado. It feels surreal. Surely the man who is about to end the world, as we know it, should wear golden robes or a glittering cloak. But no, I wear simple clothes. I shut my eyes and allow my emotions to engulf the part of my brain controlling how my actions affect the Earth. War breaks out almost instantaneously; the languages may be different, but the cries are the same.

"Death to Traitors."

Guns fire, bombs explode, and people weep for losses.

"It's done," I utter and collapse onto the floor.

"It's far from done." Pluto comes down to my ear. He pushes a knife into my hand, that I know as a weapon which can kill gods. We had believed it lost but Pluto had it all the time. "I'll have Orcus take them back to your land in Tuscany, but only after, I get word."

"Word?" I look down at the knife and up at Pluto.

"There's only one person who can stop what's happening now, and I want him dead."

"Who?" I ask, my tone laced with confusion and exhaustion.

"Jupiter. Your father." Pluto spits down into my face.

"No!" Vicky shouts.

Luigi turns around to face me. "Papa." He tries to run for me, but one of the men grabs him by the scruff of the neck and holds him tightly.

"It's ok," I try to reassure. "We'll go home soon. Everything'll be alright."

"Mars, no." Vicky whimpers and tries to move, but her body is almost beyond broken. Her inability to see beauty anymore is seeping from her pores and filling the room with a pungent mold. She's still not in control of her powers, though, so she can't see the destruction comes from her. I want to run to them, embrace them, and reassure them everything'll be alright, but I know the world has changed, now. I tighten my grip around the knife, take one final look at the two people who mean the world to me, and dematerialize.

When I reappear in my body, I'm in my father's office. He's sitting at his chair, his head bowed and his fingers rubbing against his temples. I know he's listening in to the suffering happening in the world. He looks old. For the first time in his life, I don't see him as the strong person I love and worship. He's tired of fighting endless battles for many millions of years. He brings his head up, and I see the defeat in his eyes.

"You've come to kill me," he states and stands up. His arms fall to his side, and he offers himself no means of protection against what I'm about to do.

"I have to."

"My grandson, my first one."

"He has him." My voice breaks. I can barely hear it over the sounds of murder and violence filling my head. I just want it to stop. People think being a god is a gift, but to me, it's nothing more than torture. I bring the knife up and dematerialize again. This time, I reappear behind my father and plunge the weapon through his back. "I have to save him, I'm sorry."

Without allowing myself to think about what I'm doing, because the consequences will destroy me, I focus on Luigi and Vicky and bring my father and I back to Pluto's world. The God of the Underworld's eyes grow wide with surprise when I appear and pull the knife from my father's back and allow his dying body to slump down onto the floor.

"Now, give me what's mine."

VENUS

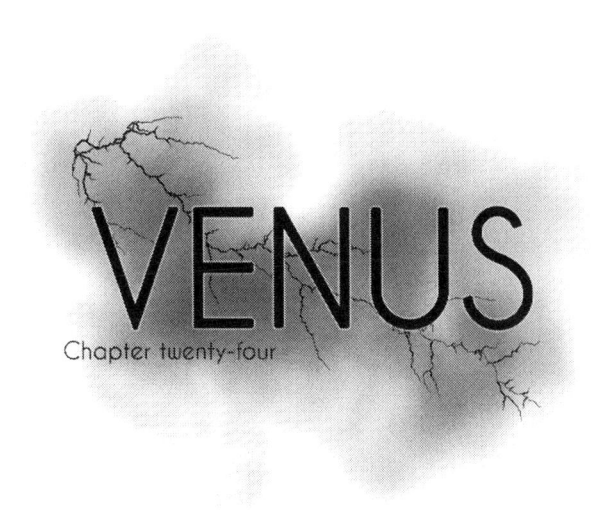

Chapter twenty-four

I can't tear my gaze away from the man on the floor. Mars' father.

Blood begins to spread beneath him where he's lying still and lifeless.

Pluto stands, gloating.

He's won.

Mars' dark eyes meet mine. They're full of pain. Defeat. He's letting loose war on the world to save us. Destroying mankind.

"Don't do this...please you have to stop." My voice cracks on the last word. "You still have time to stop this."

I don't want to be the cause of this destruction. I know in my heart it means the end of the God of War. He'll fall to his dark side.

That's Pluto's plan.

The evil male in question turns to survey me coldly. "Vicky, Vicky, you still cling to hope when there's none left."

"There's always hope."

I can barely breathe through the pain. Even the smallest movement sends it rippling through the cuts littering my skin.

Luigi's weeping still echoes through my head. The tormented look on the boy's expression as his eyes pleaded in silence for forgiveness.

It entwines with Mars' agony, becoming my own. We're bound. All three of us in this moment.

Yet, through it all, I feel a flicker of something fierce.

Love.

I love them. Father and son.

It surges up from the recesses of my heart and soul. Not something quiet and soft.

No, this is thundering. Deafening.

They've risked everything for me.

Like a changing tide, it sweeps over me, through me, filling every cell in my body with the warmth of light.

Pluto's dark devious eyes narrow on Mars. "You can have them when mankind is wiped from the planet."

"That wasn't the agreement," The God of War growls.

"It is now. Get on the floor and grovel at my feet. Show them you're defeated, and I might give you one of them back."

This monster has no plans to let us go. Even I can see that.

"Papa," Luigi's whisper is frightened. He's trying to be brave, but it doesn't prevent the tears sliding down his pale, trembling cheeks. Watching his father, a man who's been his strength, made to beg will break him further.

Enough. I've had enough.

Hate, rage, pain, love. I feel them building, swelling.

There's a melting pot inside me, fusing together to

become something stronger.

Raw and primal, it explodes out of me in a shockwave.

The force sends everyone in the room crashing back and off their feet.

Handcuffs keeping me bound to the chair gone, I rise from the seat.

Vengeance.

It burns through my blood.

With it comes power.

Everything else is forgotten but this new pulsing need.

"Vicky?"

Ignoring Luigi's soft call, I stalk with purpose to the dark-haired male as he staggers to stand.

"Your heart's a cold empty stone in your chest." Stabbing him in that area with a finger, I force Pluto back against the wall. "I can see it now. Dull and lifeless."

His lips curl up with an unpleasant smile. "Venus, I was wondering what would finally push you over the edge. Was it seeing how weak Mars truly is?"

"Vicky, what are you doing?" Mars' question is a low, icy mutter behind me.

I don't bother to look back. My whole focus is on this vile man. "Take your father and son and leave." The authority and confidence in my voice shakes the room.

"No. Pluto is mine."

Turning my head, my eyes flash a warning. I may love him, but he won't have my prey until I'm done.

Battle and bloodshed seep from him in a cloud that although unseen, I can sense through the tingling of my skin. Nostrils flared, his intense eyes are wild. He looks unhinged. Demented with something he can no longer control.

The two men who were teaching Luigi how to torture scramble to their feet. In seconds, they're on Mars.

He's grunts as a knife finds its way into his thigh. With a roar, he falls seamlessly into fighting.

Have I lost him? Has this finally tipped Mars over?

Cruel hands grip my forearms, bringing me back to the deadly God of the Underworld I still have pinned.

"You can't beat me. It's already too late, and you my dear, don't have the power to kill me."

His scoffing tone sets my teeth on edge.

"Who said anything about killing you?" Pressing my palm flat, I concentrate on the steady beating which lays beneath.

He's dead inside, even though he's living. There's nothing soft in him. Ambition and hatred drive him. No goodness. No light.

That's about to change. I'm going to give him a gift I know will also become his greatest anguish.

Energy pours from my skin, pure and golden. All my love for Mars. Everything I feel for him with every fiber of my being.

A taste of something, which can bring both joy and heartache. Just one ember. Enough to ignite a spark that will only grow.

The hands gripping my arms jerk up to encircle my throat. Squeezing, Pluto begins to choke me.

It's too late. The seed of love is planted. My true powers have finally been set free. Both beautiful and frightening. Pluto with his twisted plans has unwittingly unlocked them, just not in the way he desired.

"What did you do?" he hisses.

Even though he's strangling the breath from me, I can't

stop my smile. Defiance dancing in the depth of my eyes. He's screwed for eternity, and we both know it.

Does he feel it already germinating? The beauty of the emotion.

"You've cursed me." Shoving me aside, he stumbles from the wall. "Orcus. Kill them all."

A male appears. Huge and hulking, he radiates death.

"Vicky, take Luigi and my father and get out of here, now!" Mars shouts his intentions clear. His voice is barely recognizable, so drenched in something sinister and menacing.

I don't question or argue.

The boy meets me halfway. Clambering over the dead bodies his father has left, he takes my hand. Crouching together over his grandfather, I check for a pulse. Weak and thready, life signs are there.

"Can you teleport?"

Luigi shakes his head. "No, but you can, now. You've had your awakening. That ability will be yours."

I can? At least something I'm relieved to hear.

Mars is already battling when I look up; the need to see him like my need to breathe. I don't want to leave him. The thought sends my stomach churning.

"You come back to us. You hear me, Mars? We need you." I tell him not even sure he hears me as he trades blow after blow.

Pluto's attention snaps our way. I know, then, our time is up.

Clutching the boy and his Grandfather, I close my eyes, letting something familiar swim through my head.

"Luigi!" The familiar female voice sobs the child's name.

Bellona.

Opening my eyes, I see the interior of Mars' villa. Relief slumps my shoulders.

"Mamma, Grandfather is hurt. Please, we must help him."

"Get a towel quickly," I tell him. "We need to stem the flow of blood."

To be honest, I'm surprised Jupiter's lasted this long.

Obeying my command, Luigi dashes across the room, heading for the downstairs bathroom. Seconds later, he's back with what I need.

From her place curled up on the corner of the sofa, his mother's eyes drop to the still bleeding male. Her beautiful face is puffy and swollen from tears. "Who?"

"Mars," I tell her grimly. Pressing the material to my patient's stab wound, I pray we can get him medical attention before he bleeds out completely.

"Where is he now?"

"Facing down Pluto and Orcus. We need to get his father to a hospital. If he's a god, why isn't he healing?"

"If it was inflicted in the Underworld, it slows our naturally fast ability to heal. It makes us more vulnerable." Crawling from her position, she moves down to the floor to join us, taking her shaking son in her arms. "Apollo. Hercules."

Her call is answered with a blinding flash of light so bright that color dances in my vision.

When I'm able to see again, I find two men towering above us.

"Father!" Both gods cry out in unison. "What happened?"

"Can you help him?" I asked, choosing to ignore their question. Would they hurt Mars if they found out he was the culprit? Blame me and Luigi for getting caught? I don't know them. Can't be certain of anyone's reactions right now. All I know is this man has to live whatever it takes.

"Yes. Our mother can." The taller of the brothers confides. As he crouches next to me, I grab his hand guiding it to keep up the pressure I've been keeping on the wound.

Without another word all three of them vanish.

Hands shaking, I stare at the blood. It's not just mine now.

Everything hurts. The numbness from adrenaline, and whatever overtook me, is starting to wear off. "Is there anything you can do to stop the violence Mars has unleashed? Prevent it from making him lose his mind?"

I'm terrified he's too far gone. That he'll be consumed.

Will anything make a difference with things already set in motion? If his Father survives, will it sway Mars' fate?

Sinking down onto the carpet, my wounds throb as they begin to heal. I'm weighed down with everything. I know if I go to help him, I would just put him in greater danger.

Bellona shifts uneasily. "It's calling to the war inside me...but I can try."

MARS

Chapter twenty-five

The second I know Vicky has taken my son and father from the Underworld, I allow the true depths of the hatred flooding my veins to take over my body. Two lackey's who were aiding in the torturing of my woman lie dead at my feet. Their bodies are twisted beyond recognition as humans. I've decimated them. My fury exploding in a torrent of powerful blows, shattering their bones.

Orcus steps in front of me and blocks my path toward my intended target, Pluto. The God of the Underworld is still feeling the effects of whatever Vicky did to him. His face is pale, and a fine sheen of sweat layers his furrowed brow. He's not suffering physically, but his mind is in torment. I can't help but smirk.

"You won't find what happens next funny. You think by leaving here they'll be safe. Can't you hear the world out there anymore? Has your mind become so damaged that you are beyond hearing the chaos you create now?"

A human appears in the air beside us and falls to the

ground. When he stands, I notice his body is cleaved in half from the shoulder to navel. Orcus holds his hand out and, like he's coiling in an invisible string, winds the human toward him as if he were a puppet. The human stands in front of him, swaying. He's come from the world above and is a dead soul. Another appears and then another. All around the room, people stand with wounds that have killed them as a result of the war raging through my mind. Watching intently, I see Orcus bring his finger to the forehead of the soul immediately before him. The body catches fire and disintegrates to a pile of dust. The God of Death now waves his hand and from the ashes comes the departing soul, black as the night and destined for eternal hell and damnation at the hands of the gods within the underworld. The other humans around me all burst into flames, and the same thing happens to them. I watch them, one at a time, my head twisting eerily as I take in their faces: women, children, men, different races, different nationalities. All dead because of war.

I know I should care. I should try and stop what's happening, but my mind isn't responding to the common sense within it. It's blinded by the hatred blackening my own soul. I'm in the middle of my own fight, and that has wrapped itself around everything I am. I can't see light anymore– I know I'll not think clearly again until I hold Pluto's severed head in my hands.

The final few souls in the room disappear into hell and Orcus laughs.

"How the mighty have fallen. Your father will die; your son has lost his innocence, and Venus is scarred for life as Pluto's whore. You've failed them all, Mars. They won't want you back. You might as well submit to the darkness coursing through your veins and join us."

"Join you." My mind stutters into thought. "Why would I want to do that? You're the reason I have nothing left. No, I think I have a better idea. I'll kill you both and take over the Underworld."

Orcus' brows raise in shock.

"You've gone insane. Pluto's truly destroyed the mighty God of War."

"No, he hasn't. He's just helped me embrace the side I've wanted to keep hidden."

For someone who's billions of years old, I have perfect eyesight, but the further I slip into the darkness, the more blurred the edges become as my eyes focus on movements that'll bring suffering. Without any control of my body, I lunge forward with a battle cry. My spear materializes in my hand, and I aim it straight for Orcus. He's quick to react, though, and his own weapon, a scythe, stops my spear's progress. We battle together in a clashing of metal, neither gaining any momentum.

"Stop fighting the inevitable, Mars. War and Death are linked. Along with Pluto, we can rule this planet and what's beneath it. We can be the most powerful gods in existence." Orcus lunges for me, and his scythe cuts through the skin of my already wounded leg. I don't feel pain. I'm beyond fundamental feelings. I'm a vessel only intent on battle.

"War doesn't form alliances. It nurtures hate, allowing it to grow and strangle everything around it. War sees all. It notices the way Pluto stands back and allows you to fight on your own against a man more powerful than you, for he has nothing left to lose."

Orcus turns his head and looks at Pluto. The God of the Underworld is even paler than he was before.

"He's feeling the emotion of love for the first time." I laugh, and the eerie cackle fills the room. My vision blurs further. I can barely see.

Orcus refocuses back on me and our fight resumes. He charges at me, but I use my abilities to jump out of his way and high into the air. This doesn't stop him, though, as he twists quickly, and the scythe slashes down my back.

"I'll take you apart piece by piece if you want, but if I were you, I'd just submit to your new ruler."

I laugh and glide down to the ground. I dematerialize and reappear directly in front of Orcus. He's not quick enough to protect himself, and I'm able to run my spear directly through him. To a mortal, the blow would be instantly fatal. But gods can repair themselves from a wound like this, however, not down here in the underworld. I've left Orcus no choice but to transport himself to the surface to heal. He opens his mouth to throw another insult at me but only a spluttering of blood comes out. I pull the spear out–crimson decorates my prized weapon. The blood of my enemy. My god rejoices, and my vision all but vanishes.

Orcus dematerializes in a swirl of black smoke, and I adjust my attention to Pluto. I can feel the fear emanating from him. The alien feelings, which are flooding through his body, place seeds of doubt in his emotions. In this moment, we both know I'm more the devil than he is.

"It's a strange feeling isn't it?" I ask him, though I can't see him any longer because battles raging around the world now fill my vision "Love. It does strange things to you. It makes you destroy yourself. It will make you rip at your skin until you tear it from your body. It's the most dominant emotion you'll ever feel. Even more powerful than the triumph you thought would be coursing through your veins."

Pluto curls his lip up into a smirk.

"Don't you mean the victory that's running through my veins? You don't get it do you, Mars? I've won. You've lost. Venus and your son may have escaped, but you father's gravely wounded and will never trust you again. And up there on the surface of the world, war rages, and with it death and destruction. I see it in your eyes. They're as black as night. Your humanity has gone. This love you speak of will mean nothing to you ever again for you're evil now and incapable of such emotions. Venus may have touched me with this failed curse, but what she fails to realize is that to love, you need a soul. I lost mine years ago. Ask Prosphenia, if you don't believe me. I wonder if she'll show you the scars, the bruises, the hatred she has for me."

"She doesn't need to show me the hatred she has for you. It's written all over her face whenever she comes to the surface and escapes her hell down here." I picture the slight goddess's features whenever she captures her first glimpse of the sunlight each spring. They, immediately, become illuminated with the knowledge of her freedom and respite for six months. She becomes happy and relaxed.

"Shame when she returns to the surface, this time, there won't be anything to go back to. It will be destroyed by then and resemble nothing more than my evil lair."

Realization hits me. The world will be destroyed. There will be no peace for Prosphenia to go to. My breath captures as feverish shouts of hatred resonate through my head again. The war to end all wars will be over soon. The finger is on the button of nuclear retribution.

"No!" I scream as I point my spear at Pluto and run for

him. He sends me flying backward though the air and landing heavily on the floor.

"It's over, Mars. You can't stop what you've started. It's taken over your body, so there's nothing left. I've WON."

My body is thrown sideways and smashed into the jagged rock of the walls. Inhaling heavily, I allow my body to fall to the floor. I know my body is broken. Pluto gives me no respite, though, for he raises me off the floor and suspends me in the air.

"Death is everywhere. It's glorious. I hear its cries. That's love, Mars. War is love. It's beautiful. Destruction."

More humans fall from the ceiling. The wounds they have getting greater and more intense by the moment: burns, limbs missing, and gunshot wounds leaving gaping holes where brains used to be. I see each one's death as they fall. It's there in my mind. It's painful, more agonizing than the broken bones and cuts I have all over my body. I don't feel them. They're nothing, but each death is a reminder of what I'm causing. Nobody can come back from this. The world will be better off dead.

It's then I feel it, the hand reaching in and wrapping around my brain as it tries to prevent me from causing anymore heartache. Pluto must feel it too because he allows my body to slam down onto the floor.

"Bellona." He curses the name of my ex-consort and prepares to go after her. I use his momentary distraction to my advantage and send an almighty blast of energy straight into him. He flies through the air and lands in a crumpled heap on the floor.

I laugh. Demonic and sadistic. The blood flowing from my wounds isn't of someone who has kindness in him. It's black and acrid like smoke. Pluto will wait. The only way this ends now is with the nuclear buttons being pressed. Bellona is trying to stop it, and that means she must die.

In a second, I leave the underworld and return to my villa in Tuscany. The skies are dark, the sun no longer shines. The clouds have begun to weep for humanity. The stench of death is all around me. The vines are dead or dying, and my staff battle against each other for scraps of food. I can't see that this is wrong any longer. All I know is death and battle. It's consumed my very soul.

Entering the house, I see Bellona trying to restore peace. I notice nothing else because, in my current state, nothing else matters. I bring my hand up to release a blast of energy so powerful it sends her crashing through several walls.

"Let them die." Is my order given before I prepare to leave. I don't get very far, though, for my path is blocked. I cock my head at the vision in front of me. She glows brightly, the white light surrounding her surreal against the black filth covering my body.

"Mars, stop this," the apparition utters. I recognize the voice, but I can't place it. It's a memory of something so good and yet so damaged.

"Papa, please." A child stands beside her.

I raise my hand in order to kill them both, for there's nothing good in my world anymore. Everything is death. Death is everything, and it will come to those who stand in the way of me carrying out the duty I was given. I will protect what is precious and not allow it to be forgotten in the paths of war.

VENUS

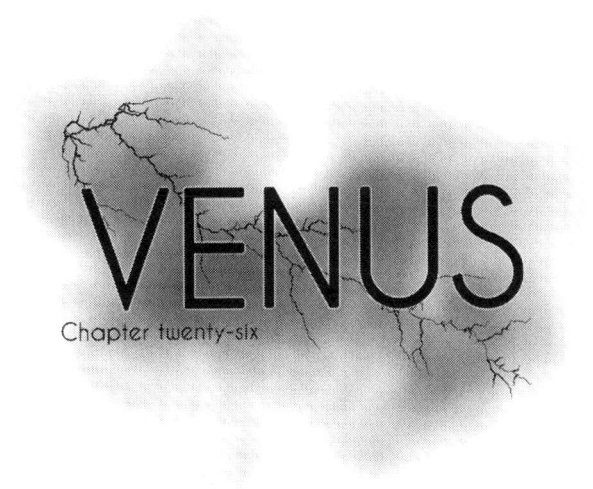

Chapter twenty-six

Mars is a monster.

So lost in darkness there's no scrap of light in the aura surrounding him.

Tears spill from my eyes, racing down my cheeks as realization hits me.

I've lost him. Pain twists my heart, ripping the organ apart.

Hatred is written over a face that once was handsome but now is twisted with rage so powerful it makes the foundations of the building shake.

The world is collapsing around us. Everything I know. Everything I love is being destroyed.

Mars raises a hand.

I know in that instant he's going to kill us. He's all instinct, now. The man he was is buried beneath primal impulses.

"Enough. Please, Mars." Voice shaky with my emotion, I

take ahold of his wrist, stepping forward until his palm is pressed against my chest. "I love you."

Brown gaze boring into mine, his nostrils flare as his lip curls up in distaste.

"We love you." I continue. Luigi is still at my side, but I know breaking eye contact with my man might be fatal. "You have to come back to us. Stop what you've freed. The world isn't ready for an apocalypse. That's something you've never wanted."

"You think you know what I want?" Mars sneers back, twisting his wrist to break my grip. Grabbing my shoulders, he drags me in closer. "You'll all die because there's nothing worthy left saving on Earth. Nothing but what I've been charged with protecting."

"And what's that?"

He falters. The anger in his eyes turns to churning confusion.

Duty is driving him. His need to see through the job his father gave him. Me.

Taking his cheeks in both hands, I cradle his face, my gaze searching his expression. "Love. Mars, you were given the job of protecting love."

A blast from behind him sends us both toppling back.

Hitting the marble floor, I swear as my palms and knees throb from the impact.

Bellona stands across the room, palm still out as another energy bolt pulses at the center. Flinging it, she catches the God of War in the abdomen.

Mars roars. The blood chilling sound rebounds through the villa.

"Mamma! No, don't hurt Papa!" Stumbling toward him, Luigi moves to throw himself around his father in a hug.

"That's not your father," she growls back. "He's gone. All he is now is a vessel of war, which we can't leave roaming. We need to contain or kill him."

Scrambling up, I hook the boy's arm, preventing him from reaching the man already rising with an air of vengeance.

"I was going to let you live. I thought you understood." Each word he speaks is low and loaded with venom. "You feel it, too, I know you do. Let it loose. Give in to the urges. It's what we both desire. Why we were born."

Bellona's arm trembles. "No, Mars. War might be in my blood, but in my soul, even I know what you're asking is wrong."

A spear materializes in his hand so quickly I barely have time to blink. With one sure throw, he aims it straight for the goddess's heart.

Only her lightning fast reflexes save her from being impaled. Casting out more bolts of energy, she sends Mars smashing through the living room wall.

"Go.," I urge, motioning Luigi to join his mother. "Somewhere you'll both be protected."

He obeys with one last frightened glance at his father, who's picking himself up, covered in brick and crumbling bits of plaster.

"You can't stay, Vicky. There's nothing left to save.," Bellona tells me as she hugs her son.

My smile is sad and small at her statement. "I have to try."

Whatever happens from now, at least I know I've given it my all. Tried to bring back the man I love from the deepest pits of darkness.

They're gone in a flash.

Finding some courage and letting the love I feel for him shine free, I turn to confront Mars.

"They won't escape." With purpose, he stalks toward me. "No one crosses me and lives. If she won't help me, then she dies just like you will."

"You won't kill me."

That makes him snort. "The world will be a waste land. The underworld will be mine when I rid myself of Pluto. I'll rule over both."

His strong capable hands are around my neck so quickly I have no time to react. The force of his attack sends us both to the floor.

Straddling my hips, he keeps me pinned with the weight of his body. Every struggle is subdued and handled with an efficiency that's terrifying. Even with the strength I've gained from the awakening, I'm not a match for this warrior.

"Mars." His name is a croak as he wrings the air from my lungs.

Gasping, choking, all I can do is claw at his shoulders, keeping my attention riveted to his face. It's going to be the last thing I see. Fate is cruel.

Fight growing weak, my fingers slip to settle over his heart. The thud is strong, powerful.

Eyelashes fluttering down, I focus on it's rhythm.

I love you.

Three words. These three words screaming out through my tortured, dying soul.

With it comes light and a sense of peace. In a wave, it bathes my body in warmth so beautiful I let myself relax into it knowing this was meant to be.

It irradiates from me, expanding through the earth and

air. I don't see it but feel the sensation. Healing, love. The sounds of violence dim, and I know mankind is safe.

Darkness drifts, poised at the edge of my mind, to claim me. It's serenity and harmony. A place I know I've been so many lifetimes before but can never remember.

Home.

"Vicky?"

The voice prevents me from letting go as I know I should.

"Please, Beauty. Breath. Just breathe for me and open your eyes. I'm so fucking sorry. I didn't...I didn't mean to hurt you. Come back...don't go."

Mars?

Lips find mine. They quiver over my mouth, salty with tears leaving the taste on my tongue.

The plea transmitted through the touch draws me back further.

Air forced into my lungs, a wheeze finds its way up through my abused windpipe.

Pain slams into me along with awareness.

Cracking my eyes open, I find the God of War on his knees before me.

He's crying. Huge sobs rack his muscled body as he hunches, head buried in his hands, mourning. "What have I done? Vicky."

Gone is the rage. The thirst for battle and blood.

Before me now is a broken man.

Reaching out, my fingers find his firm thigh to caress gently. I don't trust my voice. Don't know the extent of the damage that's been done, but I know I can't let him suffer.

Minutes pass before the comfort I'm giving him penetrates.

Lowering his hands slowly, his eyes red and swollen from

his tears, he stares at me in disbelief. "You're alive."

Scooping me up in a bulging bicep, I find myself in the safe harbor of his arms. Kisses rain down on my cheeks, forehead, and nose. Anywhere he can reach fast and fevered.

"Please forgive me. Forgive me." He chants rocking me, petting my hair. "I was too far gone. You brought me back when you sent love out to quell what I'd done. It was you who stopped this. Love conquered War and saved humanity when I was the one who almost ended it. And I murdered you for it. You stopped breathing. Your...heart stopped. I'll understand if you don't want me to touch you again after this, but for now...I just need to hold you. Know that your safe."

Sliding a hand up the back of his head, I tangle my fingers in his hair. I don't need words to show him how he makes me feel. Fusing our lips together, I kiss him hungrily. With love and hope. All my lust and desire.

Mars groans, thrusting his tongue into my mouth. Clutching me tighter, his big frame shudders with pent up emotions.

"Mars put the female down and put your hands behind your head."

So, lost in each other's embrace the authoritative voice catches both of us off guard.

Lingering over the kiss, the God of War finally looks up.

It's then I see his brothers, Apollo and Hercules. Weapons drawn and ready for battle, they watch us with a look of coldness.

"We've been charged with bringing you to justice for your crimes." Apollo says, a hollow ring to his tone. "You're to be contained and imprisoned. You're far too dangerous to be left out of control."

MARS
Chapter twenty-seven

I need to rid my mind of the residual darkness that's left within it. The shouts of war have tempered down to scuffles and skirmishes. but my brother's orders threaten to reignite the fires of damage.

"No." Vicky reaches out to me while I get up onto my feet and place my hands behind my head. "You can't do this," she addresses Apollo and Hercules.

"They have no choice," I tell her and kneel before them. My clothes are in tatters, and for the first time, I notice the damage that's been inflicted on my body by the fighting. Jagged edges of rock are embedded in my flesh, a large wound in my leg from both the scythe's blade and a knife bleed out. My back feels like it's on fire, indicating another opening that will require stitching. I'm filthy, covered in the dust and grime of the underworld, and I'm pretty certain I've got cracked ribs and maybe even a broken arm.

"Please, he's alright now. He's stopped the war, listen. Can't you feel it?" Vicky is on her knees next to me.

"He stabbed Jupiter," Apollo rasps out with more pain than fury.

I shut my eyes at his words. My father. The memory of the knife entering his body has me wince with guilt.

"Is he...?" I start but can't finish.

"Dead. Is that what you are asking, brother?" Hercules steps up to me. He's always been the shorter tempered of us all, which after what I've just done is saying something.

I swallow deeply. "Is he dead?"

"No," Hercules spits into my face. "Saturn saved him. He's weak, very weak. This will take a long time to recover from, both emotionally and physically. Knowing you won't be able to hurt him, again, will ease his suffering, though."

"He's sending me to Tartarus?" I know instantly where I'm to go.

"For now," Apollo answers and conjures magical handcuffs to bind my wrists.

"Tartarus?" Vicky asks beside me.

"It's the place gods are sent for punishment. It's..." Apollo hesitates with his answer as though he's choosing the words carefully. "It's a place Mars will be able to think about his actions, for a very long time, because there isn't much else to do there except avoid the hydra and flaming rivers."

Vicky gets to her feet and creates a barrier between my brothers and myself.

"No, you're not taking him. He's fine now, just look at him. This is crazy. It wasn't his fault. If you want to put someone in this Tartarus place go and find Pluto and put him there."

"It doesn't work that way. Pluto doesn't submit to the law my father creates. Besides, Tartarus would probably seem like heaven to the underworld," I reply quietly.

She turns to me and rests her hand against my cheek. I feel the love flowing from her body wash over my skin, and my wounds start to knit themselves together.

"I'll not allow this. What happened was not your fault. Pluto raped me and was making Luigi torture me."

I interrupt. "But I allowed my focus to be drawn into what he was doing to you both. It has damaged the Earth. It very nearly destroyed it. My brothers are right. I can't be trusted. If something happened to you, again, I've shown exactly the lengths I'm willing to go to to get you back. I'm dangerous."

"No, you're not. It's different now." She spins around to face my brothers. "I have my powers; I came into them. I can temper the need for war inside him. Love and War combined we can control the emotions. Let us fix the damage we've created. Let us do it together. If we can prove to you we can control this, then please, don't send him away."

Apollo and Hercules look at each other.

"You know this isn't our decision to make. It's father's. He's the King of God's, our ruler."

"Take us to him. Stay with us. Keep Mars in whatever chains you need to, for now, to ensure he doesn't start another battle, but let me talk to your father. He owes me that. I'm the one who got him out of there. If I hadn't have come into my powers because of the love I have for his son, then he'd be dead right now, probably along with the rest of the world."

During Vicky's passionate speech, my body starts to feel strange. My head spins, and the wounds close up and heal over. My clothes repair themselves, and the dirt covering them disappears as if I've taken an invisible shower. Apollo sees it happening and watches silently. All Hercules' attention is focused on the woman blossoming before us. All our heads turn, though, when the walls, which I destroyed in my demonic state, rebuild. Brick upon brick, they layer on top of each other, the shattered chunks of plaster overlay to leave them good as new. Nobody would know only a few moments earlier I'd sent Bellona crashing through them.

Vicky stops speaking and holds her hands out. They're glowing.

"Beauty," she asserts before parting her hands and bringing them out in front of her. A blast of blinding light floods out of them, and the rest of my house is repaired. Apollo edges toward a window and looks out. "I think you'll find I'm no longer killing the plants but giving them life. Take us to your father."

Hercules clicks his tongue against his cheek in thought.

"The minds of the people. Will they remember?"

The next thing I know we're out in the courtyard of my property.

I remain on my knees, knowing any movement on my part would force my brothers' hands and damage whatever it is Vicky's trying to demonstrate. My beautiful goddess strides purposefully across the olive tree lined patio. The tree's burst into fruit in her wake. A couple lie in her path. They argue passionately over what I can't hear from my position, but as she nears, they falter mid insult and face her with mouths wide open. She places a hand upon each of their foreheads, and the sullen expressions on their faces change. Gone are the frowns and lines of worry to be replaced with affection and eyes that sparkle as brightly as diamonds. It melts the final dredges of war clouding my judgment. I exhale a happy breath when the man falls to his knee and presents the woman with a ring. She immediately accepts, and they embrace, falling into a passionate kiss.

Vicky turns to face my brothers and me.

"Alright, we'll take you."

We jump location again, this time, to an ornately decorated bedroom I know to be my father's. Gold leaf adorns vine leaf plaster patterns around the ceiling and the masterpiece worthy of the Sistine chapel, and painted by the same man, stares back at me when I look up. It's better than looking toward the bed because I know who will be in it. My father. I tried to kill him. The memory of my actions flood back into my head, shame, guilt, and disgust allowed Pluto to lead me down a path, which saw the man I have only respect for almost die.

"Look at me son." Jupiter's voice booms from the bed. "Now."

I lift my head up. I feel like the small boy of my childhood. Neither my brothers nor I were angels as children. We often came up with hair-brained schemes, which led us into trouble. My father was strict. He had to be when our little bodies contained as much power as they did. We could have created chaos just by sneezing, but we always respected his authority and submitted to his punishments.

My father sits in his opulent gigantic bed. The richly colored covers are pulled tightly to his bare chest. I can see the white bandage wrapped around where I'd plunged the knife. I swallow deeply and lift my gaze toward his face. He looks tired, worn out, and I fear it's not as a result of recovering from the assault. It's from the knowledge I caused it.

"I'm sorry," I blurt out and fall down to the floor. My head rests against the marble, the cold of it chilling my bones. My father must pull back the covers and leave the bed for I hear his bare feet patter until they stop in front of me. I don't look up.

"He's supposed to be in Tartarus."

Apollo coughs to clear his throat.

"There's something you should see first–someone you should hear from."

Vicky comes close to me. I feel her, and all the hairs on my body stand to attention. She's my salvation, and her presence compels me to bring my body upright. She wraps an arm around my shoulders and draws me closer to her body.

"You aren't judge, jury, and executioner. As a lawyer, you should know that. You may be the King of Gods, but we all deserve the right to a trial. You will hear me out." Her words are clearly spoken and full of determination. "You brought me into this. You've made me what I am today." She places her hand on his chest, and everyone in the room, including my mother, watches as the bandages fall away and my father's chest heals. "You'll give me Mars."

VENUS
Chapter twenty-eight

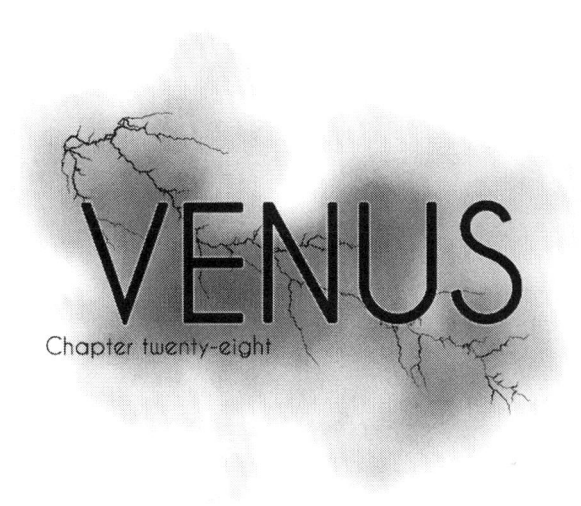

Jupiter's gaze holds mine. "He needs to be punished for wreaking havoc even if Humankind won't remember it. I can't have my sons losing control. If I don't discipline him, how do I keep the others under me in line?"

With all the strength and confidence, I now feel, anxiety still coils in my stomach. I won't lose Mars. Not after everything we've been through.

"It won't happen again. Now I know I'm Venus and have my powers, I can stop the war singing in his veins when it becomes too much." I rush out.

"I can't show favoritism."

"If you send him to Tartarus, then you send me too."

Mars' hand finds mine, his fingers tightening until it hurts. "No, Vicky. I won't allow it."

Rounding on him, I shake his grip free. "Don't think you can tell me what to do! If I have to sit outside your cell for the rest of eternity until I can convince your family to set you free, I will."

A small silence follows at my outburst.

Sighing, Jupiter rubs the bridge of his nose. "We can't afford to lose both Love and War. Not with Pluto scheming and my wounds still healing. It could give him an advantage."

"Then, give Mars to me. I'll keep him in line, and if he ever over steps it again, I will take the punishment for not holding up my end of the bargain." I persist.

"Beauty will you…"

Lifting a hand, I press it over the God of War's mouth before he can continue. "Zip it. This is my decision, not yours. You're already in enough trouble."

Apollo sniggers beside us. "She's sure gotten feisty since finding her powers."

"I think our brother is finally going to be led around by his balls," Hercules jokes.

Nodding, Jupiter's lips tilt up in a smile. "I think you're right, there."

"So, what's it to be?" Turning back to them, I do my best to hide my nerves. "Do I get your son, or are we taking a trip to Tartarus?"

"Oh, you'll have him." Motioning to his wife, Jupiter wraps his arm around her shoulder when she draws near. "You've always wanted a wedding in the family, my dear. You can plan it for Vicky and Mars in three days' time."

Marriage?

Dizziness makes me sway. They want me to marry Mars. I'm going to be Mrs. War.

The goddess's expression turns to pure delight. "That's not much time. I'll need to contact the caterers. Find her a dress. Arrange a venue…"

Her excited voice becomes muffled as I peek a look at my husband to be.

Happiness swells out in my chest with hope before it dims. I love him. Said the words to his face, but he's never once said them back.

Shock. It's etched on his handsome face. "You're going to bind us together?"

"It's the only way to be sure," his father tells him firmly. "You'll share each others' fates if you succumb to the darkness again. I won't be lenient. As mates, you'll be able to sense when the other is stumbling and bring them back from tipping into the abyss."

"Father, you're giving us no choice. Something like this should not be forced..."

"Vicky made it for both of you. Your days of spreading your wild oats are done. No more consorts. You'll content yourself with one woman from now on."

Mars' attention shifts to mine. His brown eyes hold worry and something else I can't define. Pain?

This is his punishment. To be shackled to me for the rest of time.

He doesn't love me. Affection and great sex but what I really want isn't there. I'm condemning myself to a loveless marriage to save him. The fucking irony. Goddess of Love but I won't be loved.

"Vicky, I..." Reaching for me, he doesn't get the chance to finish what he wants to say.

"Apollo, Hercules, escort your brother to his apartment and stay with him. For the next three days, I don't want any contact between bride and groom," Jupiter instructs. "Keep a close eye on him."

Grabbing both of his arms, the three brothers vanish in a flash.

My feeling of happiness deflates. Everything is happening

too fast.

"You're very brave, taking on my son." Jupiter winces, releasing a pained breath. "He's always been a handful, but I think you're what he needs to temper his hot blood."

With the help of his wife, he makes his way back to the comfort of the massive bed.

It's only then I realize how much the confrontation has cost him. He's not as strong as he outwardly portrayed.

"Thank you for being merciful," I reply, my mind still on my man. What is he thinking? Feeling? Have I done the right thing?

"I'm selfish." Easing himself down onto the pillows, Jupiter watches fondly as his wife fusses over him. "He's already given me one grandchild out of wedlock. The second won't be the case. Mars is old enough to be settled down by now. It'll be a good example for the others."

Children? I haven't even given them a thought. Half brothers and sisters for Luigi. Little ones I can adore and spoil. Teach how to paint and draw. They'd ease the heartache.

Mars would love them. I've witnessed how good of a father he can be. His bond with his son is undeniable. He'd cherish ours just as much. Of that, I'm certain.

"I want it born in the sanctity of marriage even if you have nine months left to go."

I freeze at the King of the God's statement. "I'm sorry; what did you say?"

Looking up, his wife beams at me with a happy smile. "The baby you already have in your womb."

"I'm not pregnant."

The pair share an indulgent look. "True, you only

conceived recently. A day or so ago but we can foresee you won't have any problems. You'll have a healthy pregnancy."

Mars hasn't used any form of protection. Each time we've fucked, I thought for some insane reason I was safe. All the times we had sex at his villa. The days in bed leading up until the day I was taken.

A chill crawls up my spine at a sudden thought.

Pluto's rape.

He hadn't wrapped up. He'd taken me across his desk and cum inside me.

The sound of voices seesaw through my ears. Everything around me becomes narrow and surreal.

What if the baby isn't Mars'? Would he still be able to love it even if it was his enemy's? His Uncles? It would be nothing but an innocent. Yet a constant reminder of the damage the God of the Underworld has caused.

Instead of being a bridge to bring us closer together in the hope he might love me someday, it would only drive us apart.

Finally, everything I've been holding back crashes free. Pluto taking me against my will. Susan's murder. Every second of torture. I don't even attempt to stop the tears. The misery. Feeling dirty at the way he touched me. My body might be healing with godly powers but inside it will take far longer. Mental scars I'll live with. The God of the Underworld won't break me. I won't let him. I'm a survivor. Even now I won't let him win.

MARS

Chapter twenty-nine

For three days, I've paced up and down my apartment while Hercules and Apollo have come and gone. I've not been allowed to leave as they continue to repair the damage that I did with near Armageddon. The world has recovered as best it can and the war has already faded to a memory that possibly never happened. The magic we possess and Vicky's abilities allowing everyone to heal. I tried to call Vicky once but was overpowered and my phone smashed. What the hell do they think I'm going to do, destroy the world? Been there, done that, don't want to try again. I just want to speak to the woman I'm supposed to marry today. This is all wrong. She's told me she loves me, and even though I love her back, I've not directly told her. I didn't want to be told I was marrying her. I wanted to ask her myself. It's all happening too fast, and I don't feel as though I can breathe. Maybe I should just beam myself to Tartarus, and when my father is satisfied I'm no longer a threat, come back and reunite with her. No, that's probably the most stupid idea I've ever had. If I were to do that, she'd never speak to me again, let alone allow me to put my cock where it needs to be, buried deep inside her while she whimpers my name in ecstasy. Damn I need sex. How long has it been now? Four? Five days? That would be hundred and twenty hours, seven thousand, two hundred minutes, and I'm not going there with the seconds. It's the longest I've ever gone, and given I'm not allowed to create war, I'll have to deal with the virility side of my masculinity instead. Maybe if I just take the edge off. I shove my hand down into my jogging bottoms and wrap my fingers around my instantly hard cock. In a breath, I'm tugging at myself like a freight train speeding through a tunnel.

"Mars!" My mother's shock tone fills the room. I pull my hands out of my trousers and hold my hands up. "What are you doing? Actually, no, don't answer that. I don't want to know."

"Mama?" I step toward her to embrace her, but she steps back and raises an eyebrow at me.

"Not until you've washed your hands."

I place my hands at my side and look sheepishly at the ground.

"What are you doing here?" I question on my way to the sink in my bathroom. Thankfully, my rock-solid dick went from hard enough to hammer nails to soft as a baby's bottom when my mother arrived, so walking isn't an issue.

"It's time. I thought Apollo would have you dressed?" She looks toward the garment bag, which arrived earlier from some no doubt designer boutique. With my deep thoughts racing, I hadn't had time to look.

I click my fingers, and in a flash, I'm dressed in the suit.

"Better." My mother smirks and rubs at a speck of something on my cheek like I'm a five-year-old boy about to have a photograph taken. She wrinkles her nose and sniffs the air, "When did you last shower?"

"This morning," I answer with complete disinterest.

"That'll have to do, then. We don't really have time for you to shower, again. I bet you are just like your brothers and didn't use deodorant." I lift my arm up and sniff at my pit.

"Smells alright to me."

She rolls her eyes and, when she spots something on my dressing table, hurries over to collect it. I notice the cologne she picks up and shut my mouth just in time, before she sprays it all over me. She sniffs again.

"Much better. You need to impress your wife. This is the only first impression you'll make as a husband, and it'll count forever."

I frown at her in the hopes she'll stop talking because I can see by the way her eyes glaze over she's reliving a memory with my father, and they're often vocalized to the detriment of my cast iron stomach.

"I remember when I first saw your father at the altar. I was so scared. He was already the most powerful of all the gods, and I was to be his wife. He wore his hair longer in those days and had it pulled back in a pony tail. His eyes lit up when he saw me, and the biggest smile crossed his face. As I walked nearer, I could smell the most amazing scent. It was all male, passion, and dominance. I gave myself to him that day, and I've never regretted it. You need to make that impression on Venus, make sure she'll remember this day forever."

I turn away from my mother and allow my shoulders to slump.

"She'll remember it alright but not for the reasons you think."

"Mars?" The long skirt of my mother's gown swishes along the floor as she comes around me and urges me to look at her with a hand placed under my chin. "What's wrong?"

"Everything feels so out of control. It was only a short time ago I was chasing anything in a toga to have my wicked way. Then, Vicky appeared, and I've not thought of anyone else since."

"That's a good thing," she tries to reassure me but fails.

"But it's also a bad thing."

"How?"

"Because this wedding isn't something we've decided together. It's not something we've even spoken about or been allowed to have any say with the planning."

"You know why that is?"

"Because I tried to destroy the world," I snap. "Don't you see that makes this a punishment, not a pleasure, not a rest of our lives decision."

"Mars." My mother interrupts again and places a delicate hand over mine. "She loves you."

"I know." I wrap my fingers around the tiny digits and squeeze them. "But does she know I love her. Have I told her so? No." I shake my head. "Mother, please, I know father decreed I should stay here until we're married, but I need to speak to Vicky before that happens. I don't want her to have any doubts in her head about marrying me. She's been through so much and developed a strength even I'm in awe of, but I fear if this wedding goes ahead as it is, then light will eventually fade away no matter what I say after the event. I need to tell her beforehand."

My mother pulls her hand away, and her gaze is taken by the diamond solitaire sparkling on her ring finger. She brings her other hand to it, slides it off, and hands it to me. I take it and look at her in confusion.

"I don't understand."

"Go. Quickly. I'll cover with your brothers and father. You don't have much time. Ask her in the proper way to be your wife."

My mouth drops open.

"You're listening to me?"

"I've always listened to you. You're not evil, despite what others think. The greatest war you'll ever inflict is the one within yourself. The daily battle you have against your own misguided belief that because of your name you should be evil. That has never been what your war was about. Go, now." She leans forward to place her head against my chest. I kiss the top of her head and think of Vicky.

The next thing I know, I'm standing in front of her as she sits in my bedroom in Tuscany. She's applying makeup to her eyes, but I can see the job's made difficult by the droplets of water forming in her eyes.

"Mars?" She spins around to face me. "What are you doing here?"

I look down from her face to notice for the first time she's dressed only in bridal underwear–a white bra and matching panties with stockings and garters. Holy fuck, she takes my breath away. I lick my lips to try to get some moisture in my mouth because it's gone bone dry...and speaking of bones, my trousers weren't this tight around the groin before.

"You look amazing," I splutter out, and she blushes.

"You aren't supposed to see me before the wedding. It's bad luck and all the rest."

"I know." I come closer to her and kneel in front of her, taking her hand. "I've something I need to say to you, first though."

"Oh." She pulls her hand away and turns back to the mirror.

"Vicky."

"It's ok. I know what you're going to say. It's a marriage of convenience and all that. We can have lots of sex because that's good, but you want your other consorts because you can't be tied down."

I'm stunned into silence.

"Er...no," I eventually manage to say. "That wasn't what I was going to say."

"It wasn't?" She spins around to look directly at me with hopeful expectation on her face.

"Not at all. I want to marry you, today."

"Well that's good because I have a feeling it's happening whether we like it or not. Your mother has catered for five thousand."

I chuckle and take ahold of her hand, again.

"Listen, for once. No interruptions."

"Ok." She purses her lips together to illustrate her silence.

"I need you to know that I want to marry you today. I love you with all my heart, and by doing this, I'll be the happiest man alive. You are my world, Vicky, Venus, my beauty, my salvation, my equal, and my passion. I couldn't be happier right now." I open my other hand to reveal the ring my mother gave me moments earlier. "Will you marry me?"

A smile spreads across her face the same time as tears

start to fall from her eyes. But then I see it, the moment a thought ruins all the happiness in her body.

"I have to tell you something." She trembles under my touch. "I can't give you an answer until you know."

"Tell me, what is it?" I softly urge.

She swallows deeply, more tears fall, and I let go of her hand to wipe them away.

"Vicky?"

"I'm pregnant."

I fall back, momentarily stunned, and then, surge upward bringing her with me at the same time. I twirl her around the room.

"A baby, we're having a baby. A sibling for Luigi, he's wanted one in forever. I love you so much."

I bring my lips to her, but she pushes me away.

"Venus?" I question.

"Pluto raped me without protection."

The bottom of my world falls out. The woman I love is pregnant with a child, which might not be mine but her rapist's. The doubts that must be going through her head, the emotions twisting inside her to come up with every possible response I'll give her to this situation. Would I hate her for it? Would I hate the child? Would I make her give the child away? Would I kill it? The last one feels like a dagger to my own stomach.

I sink to my knees in front of her and place my head against her stomach. Without thought, for this reaction is completely natural and born out of the love I have for its mother, I lean forward and kiss the child through her flat belly.

"Hello in there. I'm not good at biology, so I don't know whether you can hear me or not. You're mine though, whatever, DNA speaks for nothing here. You'll be my son or daughter. I'll love you as I do Luigi. Hell, if you're a little girl who looks like your mother, a whole lot more because you'll have me wrapped around your finger by the time you're three thousand years old." I place another kiss and get to my feet. "You have nothing to worry about. This child is ours."

"But what if it's different when it's born."

I laugh, my amusement getting the better of my judgment.

"What?"

"Pluto is infertile. Proserpina saw to that the first time he took her to the underworld. She wants no children from him, and nobody else does either."

"So, what you just said?"

I place my finger over her lips.

"I love you; I love our child. And if it's a girl, she's never dating."

It's her turn to laugh this time.

"So, the question I asked."

"What question? I've forgotten." She raises a playful eyebrow at me. "Maybe you should remind me."

I groan, knowing in this woman I've met my match. She's my equal in every way. I drop to my knees and present her with the ring, again.

"Will you marry me?"

She doesn't hesitate this time with her answer but wraps herself around my body and smothers me in kisses.

"Yes, yes, yes."

VENUS
Chapter thirty

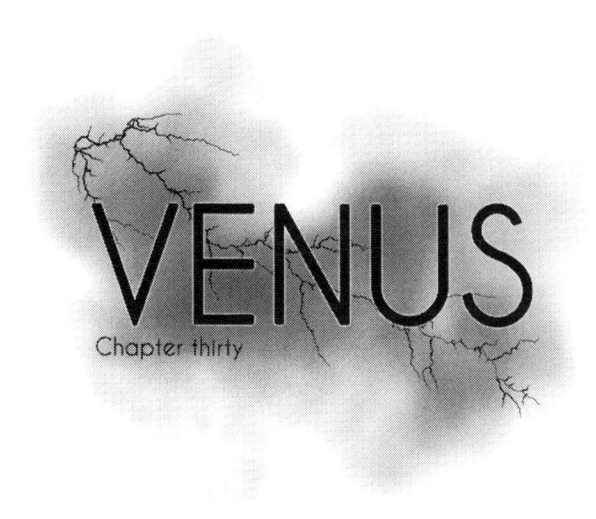

Across the ballroom, I catch my new husband's eye. The love I feel shines from my gaze, and I know everyone can see it, feel it in the energy buzzing around me. Everything's perfect. A dream wedding. The whole day's been flawless and planned to perfection. His mother went out of her way to make it a fairytale event.

Mars stands tall and proud in his suit at his father's side. Glass of champagne in hand, he salutes me.

Lips curving in a tempting smile, I return the gesture with my own flute. I can't wait for us to be alone. It's only been a few hours since we exchanged our vows, becoming tied in matrimony. With so many people attending, it's been a non-stop whirlwind of meeting and greeting. We've barely had a second to ourselves.

Taking a sip of the bubbly liquid, I recall the heat in Mars' eyes as we faced each other in front of the altar. He loves me. All my fears and worries have melted away with his pledge from a few hours before.

Luigi is beside his mother as she chats with some guests. Although he's still pale from his ordeal in the underworld, he made a handsome ring bearer. Strong like his father, it'll take time for him to heal from the ordeal Pluto put him through. Both of us carry inner scars unseen by the eye. Ones that will eventually mend through love.

Sighing deeply, my happy smile widens as Mars' mother sweeps up to my side. "Thank you for everything. You've made it a magical day." The ring he proposed to me with glitters on my finger.

"Oh, my dear, I'm happy to see you opened your hearts to each other at last," she says with a quick affectionate hug. "I knew it would work out in the end. Welcome to the family."

"To you, Venus. Our new sister." Apollo toasts as he and Hercules join us. "We expect no less from you than to keep Mars on his toes," he teases.

"Busy in the bedroom you mean," my husband replies from behind me. Slipping his arms around my waist, he tows me back into the safety of his arms. "If I have my way, you won't see us for the next century or so."

Tilting my head to the side, I meet his brown, piercing eyes. "Is that a decree?"

"As your new husband, you're supposed to cherish and obey me."

"Well, I never did like rules."

Lips kiss my bare shoulder. "I'm sure I could find a way to persuade you."

Biting my lip, his touch sends lust colliding inside me with a neediness that never abates when he's around. "I think you might just have to."

Plucking the glass from my hand, Hercules rolls his eyes. "You two love birds better go find a room. The way our brother's staring at you, he'll take you here on the floor, and I very much doubt you'll want that on the wedding video."

Apollo laughs as I blush.

"There's still the cake to cut," their mother protests.

Turning me around, Mars steals some kisses. "We'll be back before that," he promises. "I know I'll never hear the end of it if we're not."

Giggling with excitement, I don't hesitate as he leads me through the crowd across the room.

"Are you sure it's ok to leave?" I ask, chancing a glance back at the guests.

"They won't miss us, my Beauty. I need to have you now, or I'll lose my mind. I've never been without sex this long."

"Oh really?"

Tugging me through a door, tingles dance up and down my skin. In the next instant, we're standing in the deserted Coliseum. Below us, the center is bathed in pale moonlight.

He's such a romantic.

"Yes."

"Someone might catch us," I tell him, the thought instantly soaking my panties.

"The security cameras won't pick us up, and we have fifteen minutes before the guard returns from his break." Cupping my cheeks, his mouth crashes down, taking no hostages. I moan in response. He tastes of power and spice.

Walking me backward, my arms wind around his neck as my back meets the cold surface of a pillar.

Mars looms over me. I can feel the desperation in his kiss. The need.

Lips still locked, he bends to lift the skirts of my dress, bunching them up at my waist.

"Are you sure?" he asks. "I don't want to rush you. If you're not ready to be intimate again we can wait."

I blink back tears. Even now he's only thinking of me. Worried after everything that's happened.

"Please Mars, don't hold back. I need you. Make me forget and give me happier memories to blot out the bad ones."

Hands curling under my thighs, he lifts me. "Only good ones from now on. I promise you."

I don't need any urging to wrap them around his lean hips. Tangling my fingers in his hair, I urge the kiss deeper.

"You're so beautiful," he mutters feverishly, one hand releasing its hold as he scatters kisses over my cheeks and nose. "I'm the luckiest god alive."

Hearing the sound of a zipper being lowered, I squirm with the desire for him to fill me.

Mars doesn't disappoint. Hooking my panties to one side, with one hard thrust, he spears me on the end of his cock. Our groans mingle, filling the sultry Rome air, in mutual satisfaction. Pushing deeper, he doesn't stop until he is balls deep.

"My Wife." Urging me to move, he sets a rough pace to our love making, which leaves me in no doubt he's been thinking about this moment for days. "My love. My heart. I vow to keep you at my side for eternity. There's no one else for me but you."

"I love you, too." Fingernails digging into the material of his suit jacket, I ride him with wild abandonment.

Our coupling is fast and unrestrained. It doesn't take long before we're both thrown over the edge into blissful orgasm.

Panting, shaking, Mars buries his face between my breasts as he comes to a shuddering climax inside me.

"I hope you haven't ruined my dress," I tease.

His chuckle vibrates through my chest. "I'll buy you another one. A thousand dresses if you want."

"This one's special, and if it's crumbled, everyone will know what we've been up to when we return to the reception."

Lifting his head, Mars' expression is smug with male arrogance. "Oh, have no doubt everyone will know what we've been doing by the pink flush you'll be wearing along with a look of feminine satisfaction."

EVA
Epilogue

The warm waters of the Mediterranean Sea lap at my feet while I lie in a tiny red bikini on the shores of the island of Sicily, close to Masala. In the distance, I can see the hazy lands of Tunisia. It's a place I swim to often for the exotic spices and jewelry it has to offer. That's definitely one perk to being the daughter of the God of the Sea, an ability to swim for miles like a fish. To dip your head under the water and not resurface until you reach your destination is bliss. There's so much beauty in the shores off the coast of Italy, sunken wrecks teeming with fish of all different colors. Many a trinket or fortune can be found amongst the wooden structures, waiting for man to discover. I touch at the necklace I've worn since my tenth birthday, fifteen years ago. Well, in human years; in god years, I'm probably approaching fifty million years old give or take a few thousand years. Not a wrinkle line in sight, though!

My skin prickles like someone's watching me, but when I look around, I see no one. Strange. Maybe it was time I was getting back home. Ever since my best friend, Fontus, disappeared, I've been on edge. It's so unlike him to not leave word if he's going somewhere for a while. He's been known to vanish for days on end, lost in his explorations of wrecks, but he always tells me before he goes gallivanting. This time, I had no word. He just didn't show up one day. I've told my father, and he's looking into it, but I think Neptune believes I'm worrying over nothing. He has the same philosophy as a lot of the male gods have, – which is that some time away and buried deep inside, a woman of their choice is needed. Well, I can tell you now if Fontus is doing that, then it'll be the last time he is able to use his dick for those sorts of activities!

I snort an annoyed puff of air and jump to my feet. Bending over, I lift up my teal colored towel and wrapping it into a small ball, tuck it into my rucksack. The sky darkens, a single black cloud in a bright blue sky. It's eerie, not normal. The hairs on the back of neck stand up. I need to get home, *now*. But it's too late. My body's frozen in place. I try to take a step, but my legs won't obey my brain.

"She's pretty, Boss." The deep masculine voice comes from behind me, but I can't turn my head to see the face of the person speaking.

"Indeed, she is." Another voice comes just from the left of me. I have movement in my eyes, and they're able to flick to the side to see a big brute of a man looming over me. A menacing grin full of lust crosses his face. "Very pretty. Neptune should keep her better guarded. I turn my attention to the sea and will it to save me. A shot of water bursts out of the ocean and heads to the man next to me, but he holds a hand out, and the water stops and veers off to his side.

"Feisty as well. Just how Pluto likes them."

My ears prick up at the mention of that feared name. I've been taught to stay away from any mention of it since birth.

"What do you want?" My voice trembles.

"Well, apart from your virtue, you're going to make a perfect addition to my camp."

I swallow deeply, my whole body wanting to do nothing more than run away.

"But a demi-goddess? She's no Venus." The voice questions from behind me.

"No, she's better because nobody'll miss her, especially with us holding her part-time lover hostage as well." The man to the left of me evilly chuckles.

"Fontus!" I cry, but my words are lost on the wind as we disappear into nothing.

Coming Soon..Apollo's Protection.

CLAIRE
MARTA

A native Brit, I live in Italy with my husband and daughter. When I am not writing and drinking copious amounts of tea, I enjoy taking photos of my adoptive country, trying to stay fit with running, reading amazing books and being a stay at home mother.

THE HUNTER CHRONICLES

Paranormal Romance:

Frostbite, The Hunter Chronicles Series, Book 1

Dark Desires, The Hunter Chronicles Series, Book 2

Claimed By Magic, The Hunter Chronicles Series, Book 3

The Serpent's Kiss, The Hunter Chronicles Series, Book 4

Twitch, The Hunter Chronicles Series, Book 5

Blood Moon Rising, The Hunter Chronicles Series, Book 6

CEASEFIRE SERIES

Dark Paranormal Romance:

The Devil You Know Ceasefire series Book 1

The Devil's Plaything, Ceasefire Series Book 2

From Ashes and Embers, Ceasefire Series Book 3

BULLETS & BLOODLUST

Bullets & Bloodlust Series – Co-written with Abrianna Denae

Bloody Ties Book 1:

ANNA
EDWARDS

I am a British author, from the depths of the rural countryside near London. In a previous life, I was an accountant from the age of twenty-one. I still do that on occasions, but most of my life is now spent intermingling writing while looking after my husband, two children and two cats (probably in the inverse order to the one listed!). When I have some spare time, I can also be found writing poetry, baking cakes (and eating them), or behind a camera snapping like a mad paparazzi.

I'm an avid reader who turned to writing to combat my depression and anxiety. I have a love of traveling and like to bring this to my stories to give them the air of reality.

I like my heroes hot and hunky with a dirty mouth, my heroines demure but with spunk, and my books full of dramatic suspense.

DARK SOVEREIGNTY

A dark and suspenseful series set amongst the elite of a London society intent on finding power in the wrong place. Now complete.

Legacy of Succession, Dark Sovereignty series, Book 1

Tainted Reasoning, Dark Sovereignty series, Book 2

A Father's Insistence, Dark Sovereignty series, Book 3

THE CONTROL SERIES

The Control Series: A dramatic, witty, and sensual suspense romance set predominantly in London. Now complete.

Surrendered Control, The Control Series, Book 1:

Divided Control, The Control Series, Book 2:

Misguided Control, The Control Series, Book 3:

Controlling Darkness, The Control Series, Book 4:

Controlling Heritage, The Control Series, Book 5:

Controlling Disgrace, The Control Series, Book 6:

Controlling the Past, The Control Series, Book 7:

GLACIAL BLOOD

The Touch of Snow, The Glacial Blood Series, Book 1

Fighting the Lies, The Glacial Blood Series, Book 2:

Fallen for Shame, The Glacial Blood Series, Book 3:

Shattered Fears, The Glacial Blood Series, Book 4:

Coming Soon to the Glacial Blood Series...
Hidden Pain – Hunter, Lily and Kingsley's story
Stolen Choices – Katia's story
Power of a Myth – Molly and Hayden's story
A Deadly Affair – Jessica's story
Banishing Regrets – Kas' story.

Printed in Poland
by Amazon Fulfillment
Poland Sp. z o.o., Wrocław